Whisper of
LOVE

Whisper of
LOVE

Jewel Miller

HERALD PRESS
Scottdale, Pennsylvania
Waterloo, Ontario

Library of Congress Cataloging-in-Publication Data
Miller, Jewel, 1956-
    Whisper of love / Jewel Miller.
      p.   cm.
    ISBN 0-8361-3570-9
    I. Title.
PS3563.I4123W48   1991
813'.54—dc20

91-30828
CIP

The paper used in this publication is recycled and meets the minimum require-ments of American National Standard for Information Sciences—Permanence of Paper for Printed Library Materials, ANSI Z39.48-1984.

*With love to Grandma Knepp,
without whose encouragement
and never-ending supply of stories
this book would not be.*

Contents

1

Prairie Milkmaid

C AN I REALLY, MOTHER?" six-year-old Maudie Borntrager asked in surprise.

"Well, we'll see how it goes," Mother answered patiently. "It takes lots of muscles to milk a cow, and your arms are still quite thin."

Maudie lived on the wild prairie of western Kansas, in a large two-story house that Father had built. Her parents were Amish, and their family and church people spoke Pennsylvania Dutch (German). However, they used English when they visited with those who couldn't understand the Dutch. This was why they called non-Amish people *englisch*.

Yet their Amish lifestyle did not differ greatly from their English neighbors. It was 1910, and no one had such luxuries as electricity, cars, and telephones. Maudie loved the treeless prairie, their home, and even the wind that seemed to blow constantly.

Maudie had wanted to milk a cow for a long time. To think that she finally could—well, it was almost too good to be true. She skipped outside to the milkhouse and took a tin pail off a hook on the wall. Then, picking up a one-legged stool that Father had made, she went to look for Giddley, her four-year-old brother. She swung the pail round and round her head, never stopping to think that it would be hours until choretime.

"Milkmaid, milkmaid," a teasing voice called to her from the dark inside the barn.

"*Ach* (oh) you, Giddley! Where are you?"

9

"Right here."

"Playing with the cats again! You're going to turn into a cat yourself if you keep playing with them all the time." Maudie peered behind the oats barrel and saw him stroking Puff, the large gray Mama cat. "Mother said that I can milk tonight."

"So?" was his only reply.

Maudie knew that Giddley was just a wee bit jealous, and it felt delicious. If only Mother would hurry and come. She was tired of waiting.

The sun was sinking low in the west before Mother finally stepped out of the house and walked briskly to the milkhouse. There she picked up her pail and little bench. No one-legged stool would do for her.

Out in the barnlot Maudie and Mother began calling the cows.

"Soo, Lady. Soo, Bessie."

Her older brothers, Tobe, Dan, and Jake, left their work in the field when they heard them calling. They, too, each had a cow to milk. Mother told Maudie to milk Bessie, a small Jersey cow.

"What are you doing out here, Maudie?" Jake asked, noticing the tin pail and one-legged stool in her hands.

"I'm going to milk 'cause Mother said I can," she answered proudly.

Maudie sat on her little stool like Mother did and waited for the cows to come. They ambled up from the pasture and obediently stopped before them, Lady in front of Mother and Bessie in front of Maudie.

The cows did not need feed to keep them quiet, nor a rope to tie them with. They were well-trained and knew what was expected of them. Lady always knew exactly where to stand so Mother seldom needed to move her little bench. But Bessie walked just a little past Maudie. Maudie moved her stool over and in the process tipped too far and went sprawling in the dust, sending the tin pail clattering beneath the cow.

"Oh, be careful!" Mother cried in alarm. She jumped up and

hurried to Maudie's side. Bessie stepped away from them and hit her hoof on the pail, making a big dent in its side. Mother helped Maudie get back into the milking position and showed her how to hold the bucket between her knees and squeeze the milk from the large red teats. Streams of milk pinged hard into the pail as Mother squeezed with strong firm hands.

Maudie nodded each time Mother paused to explain her techniques. She was sure she could do just as Mother did. But try as she might, only small sticky drops of milk squeezed out and dribbled down her arm. Finally, she took one teat in both hands and squeezed hard until her arms shook. Even less milk came out than before. Still she tried, not willing to admit defeat.

Tobe was nearly finished milking his cow, so Mother asked him to milk Maudie's cow for her.

"What's wrong, little Bets?" he asked and pinched her shoulder.

"I don't think Bessie has any milk in her tonight," Maudie said in exasperation. She did not want Tobe to help her.

"Well, you have to know how to do it," he teased her.

Reluctantly she let him take her place and watched as great streams of milk swooshed into the pail. He patiently showed her how to close off the top of the teat so no milk could go back up into the cow's bag. Then she could squeeze with her higher fingers first and push the milk down and out. So she tried once more and was surprised at the streams of milk that splashed and foamed in the pail.

The next morning Maudie was up early so she would not miss the milking. Father, a carpenter, was out on the prairie building a new schoolhouse this week. Maudie was sure he would be surprised when he came home and learned that she knew how to milk a cow. And by Friday, she was sure, she would be a fine milker.

One particularly warm and calm day, Mother told the children they could do as they pleased for several hours. She and eighteen-month-old baby Mary were going to lie down for a much-needed rest. So Sarah, who seemed nearly grown at the

11

age of thirteen, got her nine-patch quilt top and sat on the porch steps to work on it. Fourteen-year-old Tobe stretched out on the porch swing to take a nap. The rest of the children, Dan (twelve), Jake (nine), Maudie, and Giddley decided to play a game of hide-and-seek.

Dan was *it* first. He plopped down on the fresh spring grass that grew beside the washhouse wall, the base, and closed his eyes. The rest of the children scattered, each one searching for a place to hide where Dan would not think to look. He began counting to 100 in a loud voice. Maudie slipped quietly into the buggy shed, careful not to move the door for fear it would creak and give a clue to her hiding spot. Then she quickly climbed into the buggy, a horse-drawn surrey, and slid beneath the seat.

"Pssssst."

Maudie jumped in surprise and turned to find Puff lying back in the corner with a nest of kittens.

"Ach, Puff! I thought you were a snake." She wiggled around to get a better look at the newborn kittens.

"Pssssst!" Puff hissed at her again, warning her not to get too close.

So Maudie turned around and tried to make herself as small as possible. The heat prickled her scalp and made her want to scratch her back. Just then Dan yelled, "Coming, ready or not!" She wiggled her feet, and Puff hissed at her again.

"Be quiet, Puff! You're going to give me away yet," Maudie whispered in disgust. Just then she heard the shed door creak ever so slightly. She closed her eyes, pretending to be invisible.

"I see you, Maudie!" Dan shouted triumphantly and turned to run back to the base before Maudie reached it. If she got there first, she would be free. But if Dan got there first, then Maudie would have to be *it* for the next game. She scrambled out from beneath the seat and jumped down from the buggy.

"One, two, three on Maudie!" she heard him yell. Well, there was no reason to run anymore, for he had beaten her. She plopped down beside the washhouse to wait for Dan to find the others.

Her hair clung to her face in damp curls. She pushed them back and tucked them beneath her cap, a bonnet type of prayer veil the Amish wore. Her dress clung to her and made her feel sticky all over.

Maudie saw a slight movement out of the corner of her eye and turned to see Giddley sliding out from beneath the porch on his stomach. He winked and she giggled in spite of herself. Dan was nowhere in sight, so he jumped up and ran pell-mell for the washhouse. He slapped Maudie on her shoulder and yelled, "Free!"

"Hey! I'm not base," she laughed.

He ran in a wide circle before coming back to touch the wall of the washhouse to make himself officially free. Then he rolled over in the grass to wait for Dan to come running. But Dan did not appear. The whole prairie seemed deathly still. Not a blade of grass rustled and no birds were singing.

"Oh, it's hot!" Maudie pulled her dress away from her skin and tried to fan herself with her skirt. Giddley wiped his face with his shirtsleeve. Suddenly Dan and Jake burst through the barn doors and shouted for everyone to look at the dark cloud in the southwest.

Maudie and Giddley hurried around the corner of the washhouse. At the same time, Sarah and Tobe jumped up and gasped at the greenish black cloud approaching them.

"Mother!" they screamed together. "Motherrr!!"

The cloud was boiling in anger with scaly and fragmented edges. The children stood, rooted to the ground, unable to think or move. Mother burst through the back door—then stopped—and her hands flew to her mouth. The cloud slowly began bulging in the center, and an ugly tail dropped down to the prairie. Great clouds of dust rose in angry swirls.

"It's a cyclone," Mother stated flatly. "If it comes too close, we'll go to the cellar."

Maudie wanted to go to the cellar right away, but no one moved, so she remained still. The wicked tail swung in sickening, slow arcs back and forth, back and forth.

"Can we go now, Mother?" Maudie asked feebly.

"We'll go if it comes past the railroad."

But Maudie wanted to go *now*. She was trembling from head to foot, and her teeth chattered. The railroad was only a quarter of a mile from their house, and that seemed too close. She thought of Father and for a brief second of baby Mary. But the ever-approaching storm diverted her attention, and she stared wide-eyed in horror. Buckets and boxes began flying past, and chickens half flew, half tumbled across the barnyard. But Mother stood firm, her face tense, yet unafraid.

Still the cyclone came on. When the cyclone was almost to the railroad, Maudie thought they could stand still no longer. Just then it turned due east and went whirling and swinging across the prairie.

Maudie felt, more than heard, Mother's great sigh of relief and her quiet "Thank God." Her apparent calm and trust amazed Maudie and filled her with awe and admiration. She knew Mother was praying while they faced the frightening cyclone, and she knew, too, that they had just witnessed a wonderful miracle.

2

The Brakey

MAUDIE STRETCHED to peer into the bushel basket filled with string beans. A sigh escaped her lips. They had been snapping beans for hours and hours, and she still could not see to the bottom of the basket. Vigorously she began snapping beans one after another and throwing them into the dishpan that stood in the center of the circle.

Maudie, Giddley, Sarah, and Mother had risen early that morning to pick beans and before nine o'clock had filled almost two bushel baskets. Now they sat in a circle on the porch, snapping beans and telling stories and playing games. Maudie scratched her head and yawned. Then she pushed at the cat that lay beneath her chair.

"Maudie, you remind me so much of how I used to be when I was a little girl," Mother said.

"Did you have to do beans all day long when you were little?" Maudie asked wearily.

"Of course. And I always thought that when I grew up and had a garden, I wouldn't raise green beans."

"Then why do we?"

"What would we eat if we didn't have beans?"

"Oh." Maudie had not thought of that.

"How would you like to do this all by yourself, like I had to before you children were old enough to help?" Mother asked, looking around the circle in appreciation.

"Oh, Mother, I don't see how you did it," Sarah answered sympathetically.

"Well, really, my garden was the one bright spot in my life at that time. You know how we had to live on *Dawdy's* (Grandfather's) farm until Father was old enough to be on his own. The garden supplied most of our food, and it was something that I enjoyed.

"And you know how I like apricots. I planted lots of little fruit trees and enjoyed watching them grow. Everywhere we've lived, I've planted apricot trees, but this is the first place where they died." She raised her eyes to scan the treeless prairie, and Maudie wondered if she were wishing they didn't live here.

Maudie loved the prairie with its wild grasses that tickled her bare feet. She enjoyed the mockingbirds that sang every morning. And she didn't mind that they had no apricots to eat. The name didn't even sound appealing, and she wondered if they really were tasty. Wild plums were good enough for her. Yes, that's right—wild plums and jackrabbit meat was all they needed to keep her satisfied. Absentmindedly, she nodded her head.

Giddley looked sharply at her. "I thought you'd fallen asleep," he said.

Maudie felt ashamed for not thinking about what she had been doing. She filled her lap once more with a large pile of beans. Then she looked up at Mother and said, "I can't understand why you and Father had to live on Dawdy's farm so long."

Mother took a deep breath and explained that they had gotten married when Father was only nineteen. Boys are not considered old enough to be on their own until they turn twenty-one. So they had to stay and work for Dawdy until Father had his twenty-first birthday. "Our only pay was milk and meat. We had some chickens, and I set as many hens as I could and sold the baby chicks. I sold butter, too, to buy a few clothes and lamp oil and things like that."

Maudie sensed sadness in Mother's voice and knew those years had been hard for her and Father. Mother sometimes told of the time when *her* mother died. She was only twelve years old, and life had not been easy.

Mother smiled down at Maudie, and her tiredness lifted from her eyes.

"But at least we had each other," she said. "And we had Tobe and Sarah."

The children nodded their heads and continued snapping beans in a manner more subdued than only a few minutes before.

Mother leaned out to look into the basket. She then told Maudie and Giddley that they could go and gather coal as soon as they finished snapping the beans that were in their laps. Maudie looked at Giddley's pile and wondered if she could beat him. She began snapping beans fast and throwing them into the dishpan so hard that they flew out the other side.

"What do you think you're doing, Maudie?" Giddley asked in disgust. "You don't have to throw the beans around just because you want to get done."

"I didn't mean to," she answered sheepishly, and then tried to be more careful. "May we take Mary along, Mother?"

"I don't care. Just make sure she doesn't try to stand up in the wagon."

Mary looked up and giggled in pleasure. "Go? Go?" she asked.

"Yes, you may go." Mother tickled her chin, but Mary jerked away. She toddled to the edge of the porch, turned around, then slid off the side on her belly.

"Don't you know what steps are for?" Giddley asked, jumping up to help her down. "We're not going right away anyhow."

But Mary didn't care. She followed the cat as it ambled lazily away and tried to catch its tail. Whenever she touched it, the cat jerked it away. As soon as Maudie finished snapping her pile of beans, she shook off the little ends that clung stubbornly to her dress and hurried to the barn to get the wagon.

"Here, Giddley, I'll finish your pile so you can go," Sarah offered.

Joyfully, Giddley dumped his beans into Sarah's lap and jumped off the porch—sailing over the steps.

"He doesn't know what steps are for, either," Mother chuckled.

"That's for sure," Sarah agreed. "He doesn't know what holding still is, either."

Maudie pulled the badly rusted wagon out of the barn, and it rattled and bumped noisily over the rough ground. She stopped to let Giddley help Mary sit down on it.

"Now hang on tight," he instructed her.

Her chubby hands clung to the sides as they traveled along the worn path that led to the railroad. The train that passed each afternoon usually dropped pieces of coal. The children picked these up for fuel. Sometimes the Brakey, the man who walked along on top of the train to make sure all was well, would throw coal down for them. This was a real treat, for then they didn't need to hunt for the little pieces.

The sky was clear and meadowlarks whistled around them, "Goody, Goody, Goody!" Wild sunflowers grew in the ditch beside the railroad and several wild plum trees too. Maudie dropped the tongue of the wagon and skipped to the scrubby trees to pick the small tart plums. Only a few clung to the thin branches. She guessed the birds had helped themselves.

"Naughty birds! No wonder you sing 'Goody, Goody, Goody.' I'd sing Goody, too, if I ate as many plums as you do," she declared. Gathering the few that remained, she stored them in the pockets of her dress to take to Mother. Then she heard a faint rumbling noise that caused her to lift her head and listen. Giddley heard it too, and they looked at each other with wide, excited eyes.

"The train's coming! The train's coming!" Giddley shouted as he ran in wide circles around little Mary. She giggled and clapped her hands.

"Here, Mary. We'll have to get way back so the cinders won't hit you when the train comes past," Maudie told her as she picked up the tongue of the wagon and turned it around.

Now they could hear the train plainly, and soon saw a dark object on the horizon. The three children watched and listened in anticipation. Soon the low rumbling noise became a distinct pulsation, and they could see the smoke boiling from the monstrous engine.

Maudie and Giddley sat down in the wagon beside Mary to

wait for the train. Their hands clutched nervously to the sides. With her heart pounding in her ears, Maudie suddenly decided to put more distance between them and the railroad. Jumping up, she grabbed the tongue of the wagon and jerked it around so swiftly that poor little Mary toppled over the side.

"What are you doing?!" yelled Giddley.

"We've got to get farther back!" Maudie shouted. She sat Mary on her hip, grabbed the wagon tongue again, and tried to run. Giddley sat heavily in it and made it hard to pull. She gave a mighty jerk, desperate to put more distance between themselves and the train.

This time Giddley went sprawling in the dust. But Maudie did not care. *Giddley should have been more concerned,* she thought. At least she and Mary would be safe. What if the train derailed right where they were? She had heard of that happening, and usually people got killed.

Still Giddley sat in the exact spot where he had fallen. He wasn't afraid of a little old train, he claimed. But Maudie knew better. She knew he was only trying to make her feel silly.

Holding Mary a little tighter, she could now see the windows in the engine, and then the terrible machine was swiftly there and thundering past. The ground shook from the vibrations of the engine, and the noise was almost unbearable.

Giddley jumped up and began waving wildly to the engineer. He hopped from one foot to the other, waving with both arms. But Maudie and Mary watched with large solemn eyes. Car after car went clickety-clacking past until Maudie began to feel a little dizzy.

She looked farther down the endless line of cars, hoping to see the Brakey. And suddenly—there he was—pitching coal from a coal car. Maudie waved to him. Then all too soon the train was past, and the caboose was disappearing on the wide prairie.

Maudie sat Mary back into the wagon and pulled it up to the tracks. The sun was sinking fast and they suddenly realized they must hurry, for Mother would need the coal to cook their supper. And they certainly did not want to delay that!

3

Jackrabbit for Supper

THE WHEAT AND OAT fields were fast ripening in the warm June sun. It would soon be threshing time. Father did much custom threshing because he had a machine and there were not many of them in the neighborhood.

It was a busy time for everyone. Father was far away on the prairie finishing a carpentry job while Tobe, Dan, and Jake brought in the first cutting of hay. Because three or four *boys* (what the Amish call *young unmarried men*) were coming on the train to help with threshing, Mother and Sarah were baking many pies and loaves of bread for the days ahead.

Maudie and Giddley seldom had time to play anymore. They ran errands, entertained Mary, dried the never-ending stream of dirty dishes, carried water, picked beans, and gathered and washed the eggs.

Then on Saturday morning Father hitched Nelly to the wagon and drove to Bucklin to meet the boys at the depot. Maudie wistfully watched him drive down their long lane and turn onto the dirt road. She wished she could have gone along. She stood on the dewy grass and watched until he was only a small speck on the horizon.

Suddenly she remembered the empty water pail in her hand. Mother had sent her to the well to draw water. And here she stood—idly watching Father! She hurried to the pump. It was nearly as tall as she. By the time the pail was filled, her arms ached from pumping. Carefully she carried it to the house. She didn't want to get her apron wet. Whenever she spilled some,

Mother would say, "Waste not, want not."

The day seemed endless, even to Mother. She was anxious for the mail Father might bring. News from her sisters was scarce and very precious. Never once did Mother throw a letter away. Each one was carefully placed in the top drawer of her bureau. Sometimes Father brought surprises from town, and Maudie hoped he'd bring something today.

Tobe, Dan, and Jake pulled the threshing machine out of the shed to finish getting it ready. Father had made repairs on it earlier, so all the boys needed to do was tighten bolts and belts, grease the chains and bearings, and oil moving parts. By noon it stood gleaming in the yard.

After dinner Sarah and Maudie cleaned the kitchen while Mother took a short nap with Mary. Giddley brought in extra water, carried out the slop, and swept the porch.

After the dishes were finished and all was clean, Sarah and Maudie moved their clothes out of their bedroom and hung them behind the door in Mother and Father's room. With blankets and comforters they made a nest on the floor in the living room for Maudie. Sarah would sleep on the couch. This would be their bedroom for the next four weeks, while the visitors slept in their room.

Back in their bedroom, Sarah and Maudie put fresh linens on the bed and piled thick quilts and comforters on the floor for an extra bed. Now all was ready for their guests, and still Father had not returned.

They wandered to the back porch, wondering what to do until choretime. What luxury! The work was finally finished, and there was time to play! Maudie decided to clean the little playhouse she had made in the toolshed. She skipped across the parched grass and pulled back on the heavy wooden door. Then slipping nimbly inside, she began rearranging the furniture, cleaning and dusting as she went.

On the windowsill lay pretty stones and unusual pieces of broken pottery and glass. Several wilted flowers and two bird feathers were stuck in a small jar that stood in the center of the makeshift table. But among all this finery, her prized possession was her make-believe organ. It was a frame of an old treadle sewing machine with a board across the top and black and white "keys" painted on it. She could pump the treadle and play every tune she knew.

Humming softly to herself, she dusted the table and window-sill. She threw the wilted flowers away and stood for a few minutes studying the feathers. They were too pretty to throw away. They had soft gray fronds at the bottom that turned to deep blue further up and wide bands of white and borders of black. Maudie guessed they were a blue jay's feathers.

She picked up a small broom she had made from wheat straw and swept her little house until no more dust flew. Suddenly a sparrow flew through the open doorway and perched in the eaves above her. After scolding Maudie severely, it sat still, eyes flashing angrily.

"Okay, young lady, what's wrong with you?" Maudie asked. "I bet you have babies somewhere."

But the little sparrow only blinked in disgust. Maudie searched all around the toolshed but did not see a nest. She finished her housework and sat down on an overturned bucket to play her organ. She began pumping the treadle and singing: "Mary had a little lamb, little lamb, little lamb / Mary had a little lamb, its fleece was white as snow."

The little bird chattered noisily, then flew down to the windowsill next to Maudie. She stopped playing and looked hard at it. Then it flew back up to the eaves, chattering and fussing. Maudie turned back to her organ and began playing again. She played and played, singing song after song.

Yet the sparrow would not leave. Finally Maudie got up, stood on top of the bucket, and looked all around. And there, right above her organ, was a ragged nest. She could not see inside it, but she supposed there were small speckled sparrow eggs there.

"Well, you don't need to worry about me, but if you give yourself away like that when the boys are in here, you'll be in for trouble!" Maudie warned her.

Then, jumping off the bucket, she looked around her play-house with satisfaction before slipping out the door again. She wandered out the lane to search for more pretty stones. Soon her pockets were bulging and heavy. Just as she turned to go back to the house, she heard a familiar voice calling to her.

"Maudie," it called pleasantly. "Maaauuuddiiieee." It was Mother. Maudie knew that she must be getting supper ready and wanted the children to begin the chores. Father would come home before too long, no doubt. But as Maudie neared the house, Mother's tone of voice changed.

"Maudie Borntrager!"

When Mother called her by her last name, she knew there was trouble ahead. She looked sheepishly at her. She knew what was bothering Mother, but she did not reply.

"Look at your pockets!"

Maudie looked down and wiggled the stones with her fingers.

"I want you to stop filling your pockets so full of stones or I'm not going to put any more pockets in your dresses! Do you understand?"

"Uh hum." Maudie nodded her head.

"It seems every time I wash I have to patch your pockets. Now please stop."

"Okay," Maudie said in a wee voice. She did not want Mother to stop putting pockets in her dresses. What would she do without them?

"Now go and start the chores. Father might be back any minute now."

Maudie hurried back to the shed, pushed open the heavy door, and emptied her pockets on the table. She did not bother putting them on the windowsill but skipped out to the barn instead.

Ping, ping, ping went the streams of milk into her pail. She still could not milk fast, but soon the streams of milk turned into a soft swoosh, swoosh, swoosh. By the time she finished milking Bessie, her arms ached all the way up, even above her elbows. She did not need to milk two cows, as the older boys and Mother did.

23

Next she went to help Giddley with the chickens. Together they carried a pail of corn and mash to the chicken house. Maudie opened the door and set the pail inside. Father had built the chicken house, making everything handy and comfortable. On the north wall were two rows of nesting boxes for the chickens to lay their eggs in. Along the other three walls, rails were nailed part way up for them to roost on. In the corner beside the door was a little chicken-sized door that the children opened at noon (after the chickens had laid their eggs) to let them run and scratch in the yard.

Maudie thought Father was the best carpenter in the world. But tonight she was not thinking of Father's clever chicken house. Instead, she was wondering when he would come home and if he was bringing something for them. Absentmindedly she filled the egg basket.

"How many eggs did you get?" Giddley asked her.

"Oh, I don't know—I wasn't counting."

"What's the matter? You think Father's goin' to bring you something?" he teased, looking slyly at her from the corner of his eye.

"Ach, Giddley!" was all she answered as she counted the fawn-colored eggs. "Twenty-four," she announced. "I suppose Mother will keep all the eggs for us while the hired boys are here."

"Hush, Maudie. Here comes Father now!" Giddley jumped up and peeked out the door. Father had driven into the lane so slowly no one had heard him approach.

"There are four boys along," Giddley whispered.

"Sure enough." Maudie crowded close behind him to see.

"They have funny haircuts," Giddley observed with only one eye peeking around the door frame.

"Well, maybe they will think yours is funny, too," Maudie said as she gave his Dutchboy haircut a little jerk.

"Ouch!" He jabbed his elbow into her stomach.

"Quit it!" she whispered loudly and gave him a push that sent him tumbling out the door.

"Why did you do that?" he hissed as he quickly looked at the house to see if he had been noticed. Then none too gently he crowded her back to regain his position just inside the door.

Silently they watched as Father and the hired boys lifted boxes and suitcases off the wagon. Mother came out of the barn and walked up to them. She shook hands with the boys, then walked over to a wooden box and lifted its lid. From the shed the children saw her pick up a bright red object and smell it.

"Father brought something!" Maudie exclaimed. "Let's go and see what it is."

Shyly the two walked to the house.

"Well, who comes here?" Father called to them, his eyes twinkling merrily. "Come over and meet these fellows."

Maudie and Giddley shook hands with the boys as Father introduced them. They were Sam Gingerich, Perry Miller, Alabama Joe Mast, and Elmer Yoder. Then, with his shyness gone, Giddley jumped into the bed of the wagon.

"What's that?" he asked, pointing to another crate of the shiny red things.

"What?!" Father walked over to the wagon. "Don't you know what apples are?" he asked his son in a loud, booming voice.

Giddley shrugged his shoulders and picked one up. He too smelled it, as he had seen Mother do. Father took the apple from him and began shining it with his shirttail.

Suddenly he realized how deprived his children were of the comforts he had taken for granted as a child. With his pocketknife, he sliced the apple in two and handed Giddley a piece. Giddley looked at it suspiciously before handing it to Maudie. The hired boys burst out laughing.

"What's the matter, Giddley? You scared?" Father asked, his belly shaking silently.

"Aw . . . I thought Maudie might want to try it first," Giddley answered.

Maudie didn't want to take the first bite either, but because everyone was watching, she bravely bit into it. It had a tart sweet taste and was delicious. She took a second bite.

"Is it good?" Giddley asked.

She nodded and continued to eat the slice of apple. Giddley turned to Father and asked for another one.

"There are enough here for you to eat all you want," Father told the children. "Just don't make pigs of yourselves."

That evening Mother served stewed apples along with jackrabbit hamburger, fried potatoes, and tomato gravy. There was also fresh bread and rich golden butter. When Jake passed the green porcelain bowl filled with sweet juicy apples, he asked Mother, "If you pick an apple off a tree, does another one grow right there?"

Silence fell upon the room for a few seconds before they all burst out laughing. Maudie laughed too, even though she wondered the same thing.

"No, Jake," Mother answered kindly. "Each apple grows at a different place."

"Well, I didn't know," he replied, shrugging his shoulders. He took another bite of apple, then added, "They sure are good."

After supper Father showed the hired boys their room upstairs while Maudie, Sarah, and Mother cleaned the kitchen. Giddley carried in a bucket of coal while Jake brought in fresh water.

Little Mary toddled around the kitchen following Mother. When Father came downstairs again, he picked her up, set her on his shoulders, and galloped about the house, pretending to be her horse.

Ride, oh, ride a horsie,
Half a mile an hour.
Tomorrow we're going to cut the wheat,
So the horse has something to eat.
Then we'll go . . .
Bumping, bumping, bumping!

And with the last *bumping*, he pretended to buck her off, flipping her through the air and setting her gently down in front of him.

Breathlessly she begged, "*Duh es meh* (do it more)!"

So around and around they went, through the kitchen, dining room, and living room. Then they made a circle through Mother and Father's bedroom and came back through the kitchen again.

Despite the work-filled days that lay ahead, everyone was in a jolly mood. But once the kitchen was clean, they all went to bed, even though it was not yet dark. Father knew that tired bodies could not work well, and Mother believed that "a penny saved is a penny earned," so they did not burn oil unless absolutely necessary.

Every day for the next four weeks, Father and the hired boys worked hard from sunup to late afternoon. Mother cooked three meals a day for them while Giddley and Jake took turns carrying water to the fields. Maudie helped Mother at mealtime and did more than her usual chores at the barn.

But the best part of the day was after supper when the dishes were done. Then the family gathered on the front porch with the hired boys and listened to them tell stories of their families back East. Maudie loved their quiet conversation and robust laughter. She enjoyed feeling the night steal on them in cool relief from the hot summer sun.

One evening Tobe asked Alabama Joe how he had gotten *Alabama* on the front of his name.

"Well, you see, my dad heard of a place called Bay Minette, Alabama, and thought it sounded like an interesting place to live. So we all worked hard and packed everything up, loaded it on a train, and took off. But when we got there, Dad got off the train, looked around, and decided it wasn't a good place to live after all. So we turned around and went back home. We never even unloaded our things. Just waited until the train went north again and went with it."

"I see," Tobe nodded, smiling a little. "So you moved away without moving away."

"I guess so. And ever since then, I've been called Alabama Joe."

That night Maudie lay in her makeshift bed on the living-room floor and watched the light slip away into the warm velvety night. Alabama Joe's words came back to her. She hoped Father never got a notion to move away to some unknown place like Bay Minette, Alabama. She hoped they would never leave Ford County, Kansas, for she loved their home with its fine two-story house, barn, toolshed, and chicken house. Because Father had built all of this, it was home, and she hoped they would stay here forever.

One by one the stars appeared, and deep within her heart Maudie felt safe and secure.

4

At School

ONE MORNING IN EARLY September, Maudie woke to a chilly breeze coming through the open window. *Oh,* she thought, *maybe summer is nearly over.* The fresh air invigorated her, and she jumped happily out of bed. Skipping down the stairs, she hurried to her mother's side to see what she was preparing for breakfast. It looked like fried potatoes and eggs.

Maudie felt so good that Mother did not need to remind her to set the table. She went to the cupboard, counted eight plates, and set them around the table, three on each side and one on each end. Then she counted eight glasses and eight knives, spoons, and forks, and set them in their places. Next she cut the bread and put it in the bread plate. She had the table nicely set before Father and the boys came inside for breakfast.

"It sure feels good this morning, doesn't it?" Maudie exclaimed.

"Sure does," Tobe agreed in his warm mellow voice. "I guess that means it will soon be time to pick corn."

"Do you know what I think it means?" grinned Giddley, as he slid into his place beside Father.

"I suppose it means schooltime for you," Jake teased, ruffling his little brother's thick brown hair. He stepped over the bench and sat down beside him.

"Yep!" Giddley announced. He took a quick drink of milk from the tall glass before him. His fingers were still so short that he had to hold it with both hands. Maybe Giddley was only four years old, but he was going to school this year because the teacher had said he might. He would soon be five and was such an eager learner that Mother decided that he could try it. Now with the long hot summer coming to an end, he was anxious for school to begin.

Maudie and Sarah hurried about the kitchen helping Mother dish out the food. As they were busily going from stove to table, carrying bowls of tomato gravy, fried potatoes, and eggs, Maudie suddenly noticed how heavily Mother walked. After sitting down, Maudie looked suspiciously at her. Suddenly she understood that Mother was expecting a baby.

After the silent prayer, each one thanking God for their blessings, Maudie again looked at Mother and noticed the tired lines ·beneath her eyes. Weariness seemed evident in every movement. Yet no one heard a word of complaint cross her lips.

Maudie wondered if a new baby would mean she couldn't go to school. Oh—she hoped it wouldn't come to that. But she knew that Sarah liked school too, so maybe they would take turns. Then she thought of the tiny baby they would have and hoped it would be another girl, like baby Mary. How they enjoyed her, and she knew they would love the new baby, too.

But having babies was something no one talked about, so Maudie kept her discovery to herself. She did not even talk to Sarah about it. She only resolved within herself, as she had done so many times before, to work harder for Mother's sake.

A week later, Father came home from a barn raising and announced that school was scheduled to begin the next Monday. Maudie hugged the news to herself and smiled. Jake slapped Giddley on the back and asked loudly, "Are you goin' to play hooky next Monday, Giddley?"

"Nope! I'm not going to miss even one day this whole school year," he said importantly. "I'm going to go every day, no matter what."

And Giddley tried hard to keep his promise. On the first day of school he told the teacher, Miss MacDonald, that he was going to try to come every day. Of course, this greatly pleased her. Maudie wished she could come every day too, but knew that would not be possible with a new baby coming.

Two children shared the same desk, and this year her desk partner was Elsie Yoder. Maudie thought Elsie had the prettiest blond hair she had ever seen. It reminded her of tender corn silks.

The flat desktop was hinged at the front and lifted up so the students could keep their books and slates inside. If each kept her end of the desk neat and clean, then all was well. But if one was sloppy, a partition needed to be built of books to keep the two sides separated. At the ends of the desks were thick scrolls of black iron wrought into beautiful curlicues.

Maudie loved the feel of the smooth wood and hard black iron. She enjoyed the scritching, scratching noises of her white chalk on her slate. And the large oak desk that belonged to teacher, the pot-bellied stove in the center of the room, and the water bucket inside the door with its cool tin dipper—these all filled her with excitement. Their lunch pails, actually syrup and lard buckets, lined the shelf in the back of the room.

Two weeks after school began, baby Elizabeth was born. She was small and thin, but her brothers and sisters thought she was the most beautiful baby in the world. Her tiny moist hands had wrinkles in just the right places, and her toes stuck straight out whenever they stroked her feet. She had soft downy hair that clung to her forehead in damp curls. How the family loved her, and how their hearts ached to hear her cry and cry and cry!

Something was wrong with Elizabeth, but no one knew what it could be. Mother made poultices of oats, salt, and onions, and put them on her chest. She gave her various medicines, fed her teas, and seemingly nursed her around the clock. But all to no avail.

Sarah didn't go to school at all anymore, and many times Giddley went alone. But Maudie did not care. All that mattered now was Elizabeth. Her illness brought sadness that chased all their laughter away. The days seemed long, and darkness fell too quickly. Many times Father stood beside the bassinet and clumsily, yet tenderly, patted her back.

One day in mid-December Father came home from his carpentry job in the middle of the week. With him was a tall, dark-haired man who carried a black satchel. Father had walked all the way to Bucklin to get the doctor, and his presence made the world seem brighter. Maudie heard Mother sigh with relief and noticed her eyes fill with sudden tears.

Tenderly the doctor took the baby and looked into her mouth. Then he felt her stomach and took her temperature. Elizabeth did not even stir or whimper. He grasped her hand, but she did not return his grip.

Gently he laid her back in Mother's lap, bent down, and opened his black bag. Maudie leaned out as far as she dared and tried to see into its cavernous opening. All she saw was medicine bottles and a shiny long-nosed scissors.

From deep inside its middle he retrieved a stethoscope. Maudie did not know what it was or what he intended to do with it. He stopped his ears with its two long handles, and Maudie watched him lift little Elizabeth's cotton kimono and press the round shiny end to her chest.

For the first time Maudie noticed her baby sister's labored breathing. Her tiny chest rose sharply, then fell flat; rose again—and fell.

Maudie looked at Mother. Then she looked at Father. Finally she gazed long and hard at the doctor. They all wore the same grave expression, and in that instant, in that long instant, Maudie knew that her sister might die. Sudden tears filled her eyes and she spun around, trying to leave the room. Dan followed, and the two stumbled outside to sit on the porch steps.

"Do you think Elizabeth will die?" Maudie asked, sobs nearly choking her.

Dan looked away before answering. "Naw," he answered softly. "The doctor knows what to do."

But Maudie saw tears in his eyes and knew that he feared the worst, too.

They heard the doctor speaking to Mother in low even tones, telling her how to give Elizabeth the medicine he was leaving.

Shortly he and Father stepped out of the house and stood by the gate in hushed conversation.

The family pinned their hopes on the medicine which the doctor had left. They hovered over Elizabeth in an effort to will her to health. How desperately they wanted her to get well and sing and clap her hands as Mary now did. But it was not to be.

The very next morning, December 15, 1910, their little darling died. She had fought a long, hard battle and lost. Now she was back with God, playing in the golden streets. The family reeled in grief, and many were the tears that fell that week.

When Elizabeth died, it seemed that the world stopped and time stood still. Yet the family knew they had to pick up the pieces of their lives and go on. Work was the very fabric of their existence. So Father returned to his carpentry job, the children returned to school, and Tobe, Mother, and Mary carried on alone at home.

Many times Maudie saw Mother sitting quietly in the rocker with eyes closed and knew she was praying. One day when she was looking especially sad, Maudie asked why God had let Elizabeth die. Mother looked away before answering. "It's best this way, Maudie. She had so much pain, and God knew how much she could bear. The Bible says so." She paused and then continued, "There are lots of things we don't understand. We just have to trust God, Maudie."

Maudie wished for Mother's strength and courage and most of all for her faith.

Winter came with all its fury and swept the world clean and white. The days passed with much snow and little sunshine. Apart from the usual chores, there was not much work to do. The last Friday of January was cold and cloudy. Snow would surely fall before evening.

The last Friday of every month was special at school because after lunch they had a spelling bee. The children hoped the snow would not fall before the spelling bee was over. The stove in the center of the room sputtered and sizzled. White clouds of smoke drifted down outside the windows.

Maudie and Elsie's desk was near the window, and they were shivering from the cold. Occasionally icy drafts of air whooshed through the cracks and sent chills up their spines. But the children on either side of the stove were wet with sweat. Maudie wished they could trade places. But when school was in session, no one spoke unless spoken to, so Maudie said not a word. When it was time for the spelling bee, the two girls made sure they stood by the stove.

There were two lines of children facing each other. First one side was given a word, and the person on the head end of the row got the first chance to spell it. If the pupil couldn't spell the word, that one had to sit down, and a person from the other side tried to spell it. Once the word was correctly spelled by one side, the next person on the other side got a word. They all enjoyed the spelling bees, even those who sat down first.

The following Monday morning Maudie awoke to a terrible howling of the wind. When she opened her eyes, she saw snow flying so thick she could not see the fence posts or even the barn. The whole world was white and cold.

After she went downstairs to help Mother with breakfast, she learned that they would not go to school that day. It was snowing and blowing much too hard. When Giddley heard this, he sat on a kitchen chair and cried loudly.

"*Sch-h-h*, Giddley. Don't cry so," Mother chided him. "You know you can't go to school in this snow."

"But I told teacher I wouldn't miss even one day. Can't I go, pleeese?" he begged.

"No," Mother said firmly. "It's not safe to be out."

So Giddley pushed his chair up to the window. With tears streaming down his cheeks and sobs shaking his shoulders, he watched the driving snow. It blew in hard straight lines before the wind. In the corner by the cellar door it swirled in gentle heaps.

Soon Tobe, Dan, and Jake burst through the kitchen door, out of breath and shaking snow from their clothes. They had bedded down the animals, fed and watered them, and made sure the barn was bolted tightly shut. Now they would have a day of leisure until the storm died down.

"What's wrong, Giddley?" Tobe asked him. "When it rains, it pours, huh?" He pulled off his boots and placed them behind the stove to dry. Then he shrugged out of his coat and threw it over the back of a chair. He sat down beside his brother and tried his best to bring a smile back to the usually sunny face. But Giddley would not be comforted. He wanted to go to school, yet Mother said he mustn't. He wouldn't have thought to argue with her.

Suddenly he saw the dim shape of Father wading through the snow. Because of the bad weather, he had decided to come back home. As soon as he entered the front door, Mary grabbed his legs and clung so tightly that he could hardly get his overcoat off. Then, picking her up and setting her on his shoulders, he looked around the room for Giddley. There he was, sitting by the window with tears still on his cheeks. Tobe gave him a knowing smile.

"Well!" Father exclaimed in his booming voice. "What's Giddley crying about, Mother?"

"He wants to go to school," Mother explained. "But I felt it isn't safe. It's just snowing and blowing too hard."

Father looked out the window. Then his gaze rested on his small son. How he hated to see his little sunbeam looking like a snow cloud.

"Oh, let him go if he wants to that bad," he finally said.

With that, Giddley jumped off the chair. Without saying a word, he grabbed his coat and ran out the door. Mother hurried after him and warned him not to leave the road. The words were hardly out of her mouth when he disappeared, running down the lane and away to school.

About eleven o'clock Miss MacDonald looked up and saw him coming. She jumped up from her chair, cheered, and told the other pupils to look out the window. So they jumped up and cheered, too. The teacher hurried to the door, helped him up the steps, and led him to the stove to warm.

Giddley smiled. He was at school—and that was all that mattered.

5

From Green to Brown

As MAUDIE NEARED the water pump to draw water for Mother, she felt something hit her dress. She looked down at a large, brownish-green grasshopper clinging to her skirt. Instinctively, she reached to knock it off, but then jerked her hand back in fright. It was the largest grasshopper Maudie had ever seen. Suddenly, even to her own surprise, she began screaming at the top of her voice.

"Maudie, *Kind! Was is letz?* (Child! What's wrong?)" Mother cried as she ran across the porch and down the steps.

"I don't know!" Maudie screamed. "Grasshoppers! Grasshoppers!"

Instantly Mother was at her side, jerking at her clothing in a vain attempt to find the offending grasshopper.

"No!" Maudie screamed. "Down there!" She pointed to the bottom of her skirt.

"Where?" Mother asked in a skeptical tone of voice. "I don't see anything."

Maudie cautiously looked at her skirt. Unshed tears stood trembling on her eyelids and threatened to spill over. "It was right . . . there . . . just a while ago," she said rather sheepishly.

"Well, you shouldn't scream so, just over a little grasshopper," Mother reprimanded her.

"It wasn't a little grasshopper. It was this big—and had great big eyes—and the biggest feelers you ever saw," Maudie exclaimed, her hands widening with every word.

"Well, anyway, you shouldn't scream like that when you get scared," Mother said.

Maudie was silent, but inwardly she didn't think that she had ever screamed before. She looked at the ground and squirmed her bare toe in the fine dust. Just then another grasshopper flew through the air and landed on Mother's skirt.

"Look, Mother! There's another one!"

"*Umvergleichlich!* (Weird!)" Mother exclaimed. She knocked the giant grasshopper from her skirt with a mighty swing. "Was the one on your dress that big?"

"It was bigger than that," Maudie answered importantly. Secretly she was glad another grasshopper had flown onto Mother's skirt to redeem her screaming spell. Just then another one flew past and landed on the pump handle. "Oh look, Mother . . . at the pump!"

Dozens of large grasshoppers swarmed over the rough boards that covered the well. Even as they watched, more grasshoppers fell from the sky. Mother and Maudie looked upward and saw a strange glittering in the bright summer sun.

"Oh nooo . . . ," Mother groaned in anguish. Maudie looked toward the barnyard and saw the chickens and turkeys chasing after the grasshoppers as though they had discovered a new game. In the silence they heard a sickening plop, plop, plop of more grasshoppers falling onto the yard around them. Never had they seen such a sight.

"I hope they don't get the corn," Mother said in a flat voice.

Maudie felt panic rising within her again and tried to suppress the tears that threatened to choke her. She knocked another grasshopper from her skirt with such force that it flew straight out and hit the porch rail with a hard knock. Gradually the glittering in the sky disappeared and only a frightening chomp, chomp, chomping could be heard as millions of tiny mouths were chewing up the landscape.

Tobe, Dan, and Jake hurried in from the field. They, too, were concerned. The corn was just shooting ears, too green to pick, so they could do nothing but watch the beautiful crop disappear before them. Never had they known such utter hopelessness.

That evening Maudie dejectedly milked Bessie. She suddenly sat up straight and tall when she heard a strange squealing noise. Bessie lifted her head, too, and twitched her ears in alarm. What could it be?

Then, beneath the squealing sound, Maudie heard the familiar grum, trum, trum, trum . . . grum, trum, trum, trum of the train. Puzzled, she ran to the corner of the barn to watch and was astonished to see the train inching slowly across the prairie. Its wheels were squashing and slipping over the grasshoppers that crowded the rails. A helpless and sickening feeling lay heavy within her as she turned back to finish milking.

That evening Father came home from his carpentry job. After discussing the problem with Mother and the boys, he decided to go to Bucklin the next morning to see if he could find anything that would kill the insects. The next day seemed unbearably long. The landscape was turning from green to brown before their very eyes. At last Father drove in the long, dusty lane with several tubs of citrus fruit and two bags of poison on the back of the wagon. He had gotten them from the county agent and knew it was their only hope.

The whole family immediately set to work stirring the poison into the tubs of citrus. Then they drove out across the fields and scattered the poisoned fruit along the fences. They enjoyed listening to the grasshoppers jumping on the little oranges and lemons and devouring them in minutes. But alas, the poison was too late to save the crops. Not a green blade of grass or stalk of corn was spared. Only one ear of corn could be found in the entire field, and it was a small one. The destruction covered the entire prairie, afflicting everyone.

The next Sunday their church service was held in the home of Abe Coblentz. They did not have a church building but met in the Amish homes. After singing two songs, the minister, Jacob Miller, rose to his feet and stood in the doorway between the living room, where the adults sat, and a bedroom, where the youth were listening.

"Brothers and sisters," he spoke in comforting tones, "all

things work together for good to them that love God, to them who are the called according to his purpose" (Romans 8:28).

The congregation listened with aching hearts, disappointment etched deeply on their faces.

"Do not think of this as a punishment for sin, but rather as a blessing from God. Anything that draws our hearts closer to God is a blessing," Jacob continued.

Maudie listened attentively. Usually she was not able to understand much of what the minister said, for he spoke in High German and in a hurried and clipped manner. But today he spoke in everyday Pennsylvania Dutch, and time passed quickly. He encouraged them to look to God for help during this time of hardship.

Almost before Maudie realized it, the closing prayer and songs were over, and the benches were being pushed back against the walls. She rose stiffly and walked outside to be with her friends. A long table was stretched out in the kitchen, and hot bean soup was placed upon it along with tomatoes, pickled beets, and fresh bread.

The children ate first, then the menfolk and teenage boys, and last of all, the women and girls. They lingered over the meal and talked pleasantly. If a stranger had looked in on them there, he would not have guessed that they had just experienced one of the most crushing disappointments of the year. In their hearts they knew that God was in control, and they felt at peace. They would pull together as a community. The little children ran and played in the yard, and all too soon it was time for the Borntragers to leave.

As the family headed homeward, Jake said, "You can't guess what Mose Troyer did today."

"It's hard telling," Sarah replied.

"He took us boys out to their buggy and showed us a little cardboard box that had two dead grasshoppers in it. And they were every bit of six inches long!"

"Why?" Maudie asked.

"He said he's going to send it to Michigan to his brother Dave and tell him that that's what our team of horses looks like out here in Kansas."

"Oh my!" Sarah exclaimed. "Why—they'll stink by the time they get there."

"That's what somebody else told him, and he said that all workhorses stink a little."

"Oh. . . ." Maudie groaned, shaking her head, but the boys doubled over with laughter. And soon Maudie and Sarah had to join them. Somehow, attending church lifted their spirits, and today was no exception. Even Father smiled, in spite of the fact that his crop of corn was destroyed. Even though it would be impossible to feed his present herd of livestock without it, he knew they would manage somehow. They might have to sell some of the cows and calves, but they would not go hungry. With the help of God and his family, they would survive.

Several weeks passed, and again it was Sunday morning. Church was held at the David Borntrager home, north of Bucklin. While the congregation was sitting in the living room, they noticed a thick cloud of black smoke rising to the east of them.

They watched and wondered what could possibly be burning at that time of the year, for the prairie was quite dry. No one in their right mind would light a fire in these conditions, and certainly not on a Sunday. Soon all eyes were on the smoke, and Jacob stopped his sermon to question whether it was serious.

"It looks like it might be at our house," Maudie's Uncle Dan said as he rose to his feet and looked worriedly out of the window. Black columns of smoke billowed up from the prairie and swept southward.

Aunt Fanny gasped and hurried to the bedroom for her bonnet and those of her daughters, Sadie and Lizzie. The little girls clutched tightly to their mother's skirt, making it almost impossible for her to get the baby.

"We left that cowboy at home, and he must have had trouble," Dan mumbled as he grabbed their boy's hand.

"Why did you have a cowboy at your house?" Jacob asked.

"He's my nephew, but he's been out West for a long time

cowboying. He just showed up at our place Friday and didn't want to come to church this morning, so I told him he could stay at home," he informed his curious friends. "I sure wonder what happened," he added as he hurried through the doorway.

In an instant everyone came to life. Church forgotten, men ran to the barn to get their horses, mothers grabbed their babies, and the older children scurried here and there, frightened and confused.

"Come here, Maudie," Mother called.

"What?" Maudie asked with wide, wondering eyes.

"Take my diaper bag while I get Mary and go on out to the front porch. But be careful to stay out of other people's way. And don't go to the buggy until I come."

"What's burning?" Maudie asked.

"We don't know. Now go on, Maudie. You can ask questions later."

The children piled into the backseat and sat quietly. Father helped Mother into the buggy before running around to the other side. He jumped into the front seat with such force the buggy rocked up and down and back and forth, causing Dolly to stumble and step back a few steps. Father cracked the reins over her back, and she jerked forward at a run, with small stones flying from beneath the wheels. Fear clutched at Maudie's throat, making it hard to swallow.

Now they could see that it was, indeed, Uncle Dan's house that was burning. The flames shot high into the air. Fierce black smoke billowed upward, boiling angrily before sweeping out and over the prairie.

Dolly grew nervous and jumped sideways at every loose stone in the road or when someone spoke. Father slapped the reins unmercifully over her back, trying to urge her on. Just as they neared Uncle Dan's property, they gasped in horror as the roof buckled inward and then, with a great shower of sparks, crashed to the floor.

Father jumped from the buggy and ran fast toward the house. Maudie was afraid that he would go inside. But then he turned toward the barn, and for the first time Maudie saw Aunt Fanny and the children standing safely behind it. In another instant the rest of the family jumped from the buggy, too, and ran toward them. Only Tobe had the presence of mind to tie Dolly to a fence post.

Maudie wondered where Uncle Dan was. She looked around and then saw him close by the house, peering into the flames. Fanny was crying and tried to tell Father what had happened, but Maudie could not understand much of what she said. She heard others murmur something about a tramp.

"Did a tramp burn their house down?" Maudie asked Sarah.

"I don't know. It must've been that cowboy Uncle Dan talked about. I couldn't hear what Aunt Fanny said."

Father looked toward the house where the fire raged fearfully, then suddenly ran to join Uncle Dan. Maudie's heart jumped to her throat. They were much too close for safety, and she was afraid that more of the house would tumble down. How she wished they would step back!

"Oh! . . . It's just terrible! It's just terrible!" Aunt Fanny wailed in a singsong voice.

Mother put her arm around her shoulders and tried to console her. But she only wailed louder. Father and Uncle Dan came back, shaking their heads sadly.

"There's no life in there," Uncle Dan told them, and Maudie saw tears trembling on his eyelids. "Don't take it so hard, Fanny."

Maudie reached out and touched Father's rough hand. "Was there somebody in there?" she asked him.

"Yes, Maudie," he answered in a low voice. "There was a tramp in there."

"Did he get burned up?"

"Yes."

"Why didn't he get out?"

"He didn't want to."

Maudie was appalled! She couldn't imagine anyone wanting to burn up. She wondered if he lit the fire on purpose. He must have, for how else would it have started while Uncle Dan's were at church?

Poor Aunt Fanny! And Sadie and Lizzie. Now all their belongings were gone. Their dishes, clothes, beds, and all their food. They had some furniture that had been passed down for several generations, things they had brought all the way from Ohio, and now they were burned up. And just because of that tramp! Maudie could hardly believe that anyone would do such a thing.

She listened intently as Aunt Fanny again tried to speak. Her voice was now more calm and easier to understand.

"He came Friday morning and seemed so nervous and acted real strange." She sniffled and with shaking hands wiped her nose and eyes with a rumpled handkerchief. "This morning we asked him to come to church with us, but he said he was too tired and wondered if he could just rest here while we're gone. You know, we never thought he might do something like this."

People crowded close to hear her words.

"The corner there by the bedroom was really burning fast when we got here," Uncle Dan took up where she left off. "I tried my best to go in and get him, but I just couldn't." He paused as he remembered the horror of discovering their home in flames and not knowing where his nephew was.

"I ran around to the bedroom and called to him. Then through the flames I saw him lying on a pile of coal that was on top of the bed with some kerosene cans standing beside him. I think he was dead then already."

Aunt Fanny added, "Dan called to him to come out but he never answered him. He screamed as loud as he could, but the boy never made a sound." Wearily, she rubbed a grimy hand over her eyes as though to wipe away the memories and regrets. "If only we hadn't left him here alone."

"You didn't know he'd do this, Fanny," Father reassured her in a gruff voice. "Why don't you go home with Mother and the girls now. The boys and I will stay and help Dan with the chores. Tomorrow we'll come back with others and clean up. Then the church will get together and build a house for you."

Maudie squeezed into the backseat of the buggy between Sarah and Giddley and held Sadie on her lap. Even after they were far away from the burning house, she still seemed to hear the crackling and roaring of the flames. She closed her eyes to shut out the memories, but then the orange and yellow flames seemed to dance before her.

Maudie shifted her position and stared unseeingly across the flat prairie. She blinked her stinging eyes and tried to swallow the lump in her throat. Maudie wanted to cry.

6

A Noisy Contraption

MAUDIE, MAUDIE! Wake up!"

Maudie stirred and sleepily opened her eyes to see Sarah bending over her. She rolled over and noticed through the window that the sky was still dark, so she closed her eyes again.

"Maudie, you must get up," Sarah insisted. She gently shook Maudie's shoulder. "Mother had a baby last night."

Maudie's eyes flew open and she struggled to sit up. "What? Er . . . um . . . a baby?" She rubbed her eyes and swung her feet over the side of the bed.

"Yes, Mother had a baby and it's a girl."

"Is she going to be all right?" Maudie asked.

"It looks like it. She's not crying anyhow."

Maudie yanked her dress over her head and pulled on her stockings.

"Where are my shoes?" she asked.

"Right here," Sarah handed her shoes to her. "Come down right away and help me get breakfast ready. The boys will soon be getting up."

"Brrr, it's cold." Maudie's teeth chattered as she hurriedly pulled the blankets and quilt over her bed and straightened the pillows. Then she skipped downstairs. All was quiet in the kitchen. Father sat at the table with his head resting on his arms.

"Shhh," Sarah whispered to Maudie. "He's been up all night."

But Father had heard her coming and lifted his head. He smiled and asked Maudie if she would like to see her baby sister.

"Of course," she replied, grinning from ear to ear.

Scraping back his chair, he stood, and his large frame seemed to fill the entire room. He stopped at the bedroom door and listened. Hearing low voices, he quietly opened it and looked inside. Lizzie Troyer, who lived across the railroad, was watching over Mother with sleeves rolled up and sweat beads glistening on her forehead. She motioned for him to enter.

Father stooped over the cradle and lifted the tiny bundle from it, explaining that the girls wanted to see her. Maudie stretched up on tiptoes to see, so Father lowered the baby to her level.

"Ohhh!" Maudie whispered. She stroked the tiny face and felt her dark, damp hair. "What's her name?"

"Mother says it's Lydia. After Grandma Yoder."

"I like Lydia," Sarah said.

"Me too," Maudie nodded.

"Then Lydia it is," he answered. His large, rough hands tightened the soft cotton blanket around his newborn daughter. Gently he took her back to the cradle, then went upstairs to wake the boys. She heard him shouting "Merry Christmas" in a loud, happy voice. He shook and rattled the doorknob until it sounded as though it were coming off. "You have a new sister, boys!" he added.

"Oh! Is it Christmas Day?" Maudie asked Sarah, her hand poised in midair.

"Yeah. Did you forget?"

"I guess so."

Sarah never forgot Christmas Day and usually had a little gift for everyone. Maudie felt embarrassed to have forgotten it again. Next year she would be sure to make something.

"Isn't it special to have a baby on Christmas Day? That's the best Christmas present ever!" Maudie exclaimed. A warm glow filled her.

Soon her brothers filed down the stairs. They, too, wanted to see the baby. So Father brought her out to the kitchen again. They each took turns holding her, and she lay still in their arms, never crying or squirming. She had soft pink cheeks and was the picture of health. Father seemed extra pleased with her, probably because Elizabeth had been so sickly.

The sky began to lighten in the east, so the boys and Father quickly ate breakfast and went outside to chore. Lizzie came out of the bedroom and sank tiredly into a chair beside the table.

Sarah prepared a plate of eggs and biscuits and gravy for her.

"Will Mother be okay?" Sarah asked Lizzie.

"Oh yes. She's resting now and should be feeling much better by evening. Do you think you can take care of things the next few days?"

"Yeah. I've got Maudie and Giddley to help, and with it being winter, there's not a whole lot to do," Sarah replied.

"Then I think I'll go home and check back with you toward the end of the week."

As the days passed, Mother began getting up more and more but did not take on household duties until the baby was about ten days old. Little Lydia slept and slept, waking only to be fed. Mother regained her strength quickly, and the baby grew fair and chubby.

One day Father returned from Bucklin with news that their English neighbors to the east, the Powells, had a new baby in their house, too. He had stopped there on his way home, and Mr. Powell told him about the birth and that the baby was tiny and sickly. He said he was nearly ready to call the doctor.

Several mornings later, soon after breakfast, both Mr. and Mrs. Powell rode into their yard in their fancy carriage with their two yellow-spotted horses.

"Here come *Lattwarick un Kees* (apple butter and cheese)," Giddley yelled as he ran to the porch to welcome them inside. Their horses were yellow, the color of cheese, with large brown spots like apple butter, so the children had given them that nickname. Mrs. Powell came up the steps to the front porch.

"Come in," Giddley invited her as he opened the door wide.

"Is your mother here?" she asked, stepping hesitantly inside. In her arms, she held a tiny baby wrapped in a beautiful crocheted shawl. It was blue with a yellow border.

"I'll go get her."

Giddley ran to the bedroom where Mother was nursing Lydia. "Mrs. Powell is here and wants to talk to you."

Mother laid Lydia in her cradle and went to the front door to meet her neighbor.

"Good morning, Mrs. Powell," she greeted her. "How is the baby doing?"

"Not very well," she replied wearily. "Mr. Powell went after the doctor last night, and he said I must find someone who can nurse my baby part of the time. The doctor's afraid he might die if he doesn't get some mother's milk and gain some weight soon."

"Come inside and sit down," Mother invited her.

After they were seated, Mother took the Powell's little baby in her arms and stroked his pale cheeks. She saw the pitifully thin arms and legs and his sunken eyes. He puckered up his face and tried to cry.

Mother's heart ached for him and Mrs. Powell. How well she knew the hopelessness of caring for an ailing child. Tears pricked her eyelids as she turned to her neighbor again.

"I'd be glad to nurse him for you," she said softly. "Giddley, go tell Mr. Powell that he can go to the toolshed where Father is and pass the time with him while I nurse their baby."

She turned to Mrs. Powell and asked her to come back to the bedroom with her. "I just finished nursing my baby, but I think I might have some milk left."

Mrs. Powell stooped over the cradle, admiring baby Lydia. How healthy she looked in comparison to her son! She then sat on the edge of the bed to visit while Mother fed her son.

She told of the weariness that came from caring for her baby, and of the fear that clutched at her heart every single day. Mrs. Powell longed for several hours of uninterrupted sleep. Yet if the baby slept, she was afraid he would not wake again. So the fear kept her from really resting.

How well Mother knew of what she spoke! How well she remembered the bone weariness, the heartless grave, and the numbing grief. She would do all she could to keep her neighbor

48

from experiencing what she had.

"Can you bring him back this evening?" Mother asked.

"Yes, we can. How often do you think you can feed him?"

"Well, I have plenty of milk, and Lydia is a contented baby. So why don't we try it every morning and every night."

"But your baby has to have her milk, too, and I don't want her to get sick."

"We'll watch everything real close and see how she takes it. Usually the more you nurse, the more milk you have. So I should pick up in my supply in a couple of days. Let's try it once."

So every morning and evening one of the Powells brought their little baby to Mother to be fed. Soon he began gaining in strength and color. Mother decided to try feeding him at noon, too, and before long she had two little babies growing and cooing contentedly. Then as spring passed into summer, the Powells brought their baby less and less until he was coming to be fed only at noon.

Many times the children saw Mr. Powell drive past in his fine carriage, pulled by his brown and yellow horses. One day Sarah, Maudie, and Giddley were sitting on the front porch snapping green beans when they heard a strange noise over the slight rise in the road. It seemed to be coming from the direction of the Powells.

They lifted their heads and listened. To their utter astonishment and wonder, the noise grew louder and louder until a strange-looking carriage came put, put, putting over the hilltop. Sitting proudly in the seat was Mr. Powell. The carriage rolled along past their house without being pulled by the yellow horses, or any horse, for that matter. It seemed to roll along on its own. Mr. Powell waved merrily, but they were too amazed to return his wave.

"Mother! Mother! Come look at what Mr. Powell is riding," Maudie cried excitedly.

"He . . . he . . . he'll not be able to go . . . go . . . go home again in that thing 'cause he can't make it roll back up the hill!" Giddley stuttered.

"I don't see how he can keep going so long across the prairie either," Sarah added. "You'd think he would have lost his speed a long time ago."

"I know," Maudie agreed. They were puzzled.

Mother stepped out onto the porch and strained her eyes to see him. By this time he was far away, and only a faint humming sound could be heard.

"We'll see what that thing is when they bring the baby tomorrow," she told them.

That evening while they were out in the barnyard choring, they again heard the strange noise of Mr. Powell's carriage.

"Come quick, come quick, Dan and Jake!" Giddley shouted. "Maudie, go in the barn and tell Father and Tobe to come look at Mr. Powell."

The rumbling grew louder and louder until the animals began growing nervous. The children ran out to the road, waiting for their neighbor to ride by.

"Get back!" Maudie warned. But the boys would not listen.

"He'll not be able to get back up the hill, will he?" Giddley asked the older boys.

"Naw," Tobe and Jake answered together.

"Well, I think he can," Sarah disagreed. "He went all the way across the prairie without being pulled, and plumb out of sight."

"Yeah, I think he can, too," Father said, "because I've heard about these horseless carriages, and they can go anywhere a horse can. But they have their own power and don't need anything to pull them."

The noisy contraption was drawing closer and closer, and Maudie wished the others wouldn't be so near to the road. Mother joined them, with Lydia in her arms and Mary clinging to her skirt. As Mr. Powell came closer, he slowed the machine until it stopped before them.

It was painted shiny black, and Maudie could see herself reflected in it. She moved a little to one side until she was directly in front of the door. Was she really as fat as her reflection appeared? She pushed a stray strand of hair from her eyes, and as she did that, she saw how short her arm looked shining in the carriage door. She lifted one leg and giggled. It looked as if it were only six inches long.

"Oh, look how fat I am." She tugged on Giddley's arm.

They laughed at their reflections in the shiny black paint. Everyone looked short and fat. Giddley walked around to the brass lights that were bolted on the smooth black fenders and looked deep inside the round globes. Then he kicked the rubber tires.

"You want a ride?" Mr. Powell shouted above the noise of the engine. He was grinning from ear to ear.

Maudie backed up. She certainly would not take a ride in that thing.

"Do you children want a ride?" Father asked them.

They only stared.

"Do you, or don't you?" he asked again.

They shook their heads and backed up.

"Why don't you come with me, Crist?" Mr. Powell asked.

"Should I?" Father turned to Mother.

She laughed. "Go if you want to."

So Father gingerly climbed onto the seat beside Mr. Powell. There was almost not enough room for the two men on one seat, but Mr. Powell scooted over. Although they crowded both sides of the seat, they managed to sit comfortably. Mr. Powell reached down and moved a stick that projected from the floorboard. With his foot, he pushed on a pedal, and the carriage began to move. The children stepped back even farther, and Father looked up and waved at his family.

"It's not going to go up that hill. You just watch," Dan said.

"I know," Giddley agreed. "With Father and Mr. Powell both on that thing, there's no way it can pull them up the hill."

But it did. Soon the two men were out of sight. The children were astonished. To think that something could go uphill without anything pulling it! It couldn't be possible! But yet, that was what they had just seen happen.

They waited a long time before Mr. Powell and Father came chugging down over the hill again and slowed to a stop. Father and Mr. Powell were laughing loudly. The engine began sputtering and coughing, so Mr. Powell pushed on a little pedal on the floorboard, and a smelly smoke poured out of a pipe in the back.

"Phewww!" Maudie and Sarah wrinkled their noses and turned away.

The boys scoffed at them and said it smelled good. To tease the girls, Mr. Powell stepped on the pedal some more.

"Stop it!" Maudie yelled.

"No! Do it again, do it again!" Giddley screamed, jumping up and down with excitement.

So Mr. Powell sent out more clouds of smoke before moving the stick on the floorboard and turning the carriage around in their lane. Then he waved good-bye and chugged back up the hill toward his home.

Never again would the children see Mr. Powell's horses that reminded them of *Lattwarick un Kees*. Now he had a horseless carriage and wouldn't need horses anymore.

7

On the Move

IT WAS A COOL, FOGGY morning in late September of 1913. Maudie was ten years old now, and she was mechanically setting the table for breakfast. Mother hurried about the kitchen in her customary way—putting a kettle of gravy on the stove to warm, checking on biscuits in the oven, and frying eggs.

While Maudie was pouring water into tall glasses, Father and the boys clumped onto the back porch. By their excited voices Maudie could tell that something out of the ordinary had happened. Her forehead wrinkled curiously as she listened.

"What are you talking about?" she asked when they stepped into the warm kitchen.

"Somebody was milking Lady down by the railroad," Jake blurted out.

"Yeah, and worse than that, they stole a bunch of oats out of the barrel in the barn," Dan added.

Mother's hand stopped in midair as she reached to lift a kettle. "What did you say," she asked, turning toward them.

"When I went out to get the cows, it was so foggy that I couldn't find them," Dan continued. "I finally followed the fence and found them all the way down by the railroad."

He settled himself in his usual place on the bench and continued the story. "They were all there but Lady. When I called her, she mooed and didn't sound too far away. I soon found her—but—guess what!"

"What?" Maudie asked, trying to hurry him.

"There was a man sitting on the ground and milking her into a wash basin."

"What?!" Mother asked. "Where did he come from?"

"He said that he and his family are traveling through in a covered wagon. They're camped on the other side of the tracks, but it was too foggy to see them. They're from New Mexico and on their way to Reno County. He said he needed milk for the children. He saw our cows out there in the pasture, and figured we wouldn't miss the milk from just one cow, so he helped himself."

"But that's not all he helped himself to," Jake interrupted. "There are hardly any oats left in the barrels. I guess he thought we wouldn't miss that either."

Mother looked sharply at Father. "What's that going to mean?"

"Well, it'll probably mean we'll need to buy a little to tide us over until spring. We can sell one of the cows, too, to stretch the feed."

"But we need all the butter and cream we can get," Mother reminded him.

"I know. But we'll make it somehow." He scraped his chair up to the table, and Mother turned back to the stove. She knew by his manner that nothing more should be said about it. Father was always willing to help their neighbors, and if it was someone traveling through, they were no exception.

Breakfast was eaten in a solemn mood. Even the children realized that the loss of the oats was a terrible setback in an already lean year.

The days passed into winter, and a hard winter it was. The relentless wind howled around the house, nearly burying it in great drifts of snow. The supply of grain and hay dwindled with each passing day. Before spring arrived, not only one cow had been sold, but three. Now only Lady, Bessie, Mool, and Rose were left, and there was hardly enough grain to feed them.

One day Father came home from work and went straight to the kitchen to talk with Mother. Maudie was sitting at the table peeling potatoes for supper, but Father told her to go to the barn and start milking. She knew he had something important to say to Mother and did not want her to hear. Obediently she pulled on her worn woolen coat and went to the barn. How she wondered what he was telling Mother!

After the chores were finished, Maudie helped bring the eggs and milk in to cool. She looked keenly at Mother for any trace of Father's conversation with her, but her expression was just as usual. Father seemed a bit extra jolly, but then, maybe that was only her imagination.

Weeks passed and Maudie had nearly forgotten about the episode until Jake leaned over the fence one day while she was milking.

"Did you know we're going to move?" he asked importantly.

"No, we're not!" she snorted.

"Yes, we are—because Father talked to us boys about it this morning."

"Why?"

"Because we've had such hard times here the last couple of years. You know, with all the crop failures we've had lately, and the grasshoppers, and . . . just everything." He threw up his hands in despair, then looked away.

"That must be what Father was talking to Mother about several weeks ago."

She stared at the milk in her pail. Then she looked up at Jake and asked, "Where will we go?"

"I think up to Reno County, but I'm not sure. Father mentioned it, but he didn't really say."

He picked at loose splinters on the board fence and was silent for a moment. "Anyhow, I guess we'll not have to plant corn right away." He dropped back from the fence and added playfully, "Have fun packing your dolls!"

"Dolls! Humph!" Maudie grunted. She had only Mandie and hadn't played with her for a long time. It certainly wouldn't take long to get her packed. But the playhouse—that would be a different matter. She began milking as fast as she could.

She could hardly believe that Father would actually leave this place. This place he had built. Their large two-story house was so tight no mice could get in. It was cool in the summer and warm in the winter because the walls were filled with concrete for insulation and to help steady the temperature. He had built the chicken house, the barn, and the toolshed. Surely he wouldn't want to leave all this!

She raised her eyes and looked across the prairie. The grasses were just blushing green in the silvery sun. Would they really leave, never to return? Already she felt like a stranger.

Immediately their lives changed. They were, indeed, moving to Reno County, a hundred miles to the northeast, but still in Kansas. Their family and goods would go by train, and they knew they probably would never return. Plans were made to sell the farm. In a short time Mr. Seibert, a neighbor to the north, bought it. Now there was nothing to keep them in Ford County.

Maudie helped Mother and Sarah pack dishes, canned goods, bedding, and countless household items. Mose Troyer and George Stutzman came often to help Father and the boys sort through tools and things in the barn and toolshed. Then there were wooden crates and boxes to build for the chickens and livestock.

Two boxcars were rented at the depot in Bucklin, and wagon after wagon rolled across the prairie, loaded with their possessions. One car would carry their household items, buggy, and machinery, while the other one carried the livestock. Because they would be charged according to the amount of weight they loaded, they left behind anything that was not considered necessary.

On the day of departure, many friends and neighbors came to help the Borntragers move. For dinner, they all drove across the railroad to Mose Troyer's home, where Lizzie prepared the dinner of fried chicken, potatoes, green beans, and apple and plum pie. It was so delicious that Maudie almost forgot it would be their last meal in Ford County.

After dinner she did not need to help with the dishes. Instead, she went with Mother, Sarah, and Edith Stutzman back to their house. Mary and Lydia stayed with Lizzie to take naps.

At home, only a few pieces of furniture, several boxes of bedding, and their worn suitcases remained. The empty house seemed eerie and cavelike. Maudie took an old straw broom that they would leave behind and began sweeping the floors.

Sarah helped carry the last of their belongings to Edith's buggy, and Mother made a final round of the entire house to make sure they would not leave anything of value behind. The move was real now, very real. And Maudie discovered she did not really mind—at least, not like she thought she would.

Father and the boys and several other men were pushing and shoving and pleading and shouting to get the animals onto Mose's cattle trailer. The chickens were clucking in a large wooden crate. It was only tall enough for their bodies, and their heads were scrunched down or sticking up between the slats. The rooster crowed and Bessie mooed.

Maudie could hear the men laughing and shouting while Edna and Sarah talked sensibly in the kitchen. Mother's heavy footsteps could be heard on the rough boards upstairs, and Maudie's broom swished softly back and forth, back and forth across the living-room floor. In a few hours, they would be gone, never to return.

As they drove down the long lane in Mose Troyer's buggy and turned onto the dirt road that led to Bucklin, Maudie twisted around to look back. Suddenly she felt sad, so she spun back and looked straight ahead. A strange lump rose in her throat, and she swallowed hard to make it disappear. She did not like to feel sad, and tried not to care that they were leaving.

Yet in spite of herself, she turned around once more and looked long and hard at all Father had built: the house, the toolshed and barn, the little chicken house, and then at the railroad where she and Giddley had picked up many, many pieces of coal. She swallowed and blinked hard, then looked straight ahead. She wondered if she would be afraid to ride the train.

At the depot, the men unloaded the cattle and chickens onto the boxcar and put a makeshift fence between them. Last of all. they loaded the horses, Cap and Dolly. Tobe settled down in the boxcar for the long ride to their new home. He would have to ride with the animals to take care of them on the trip. Maudie wished he could ride with them in the passenger car. But someone had to take care of the animals, and Tobe was the oldest, so the job naturally fell to him.

After tearful good-byes and many good wishes, the Borntrager family boarded the passenger car to wait for its departure. Giddley plopped, exhausted, into the seat beside Maudie. But she didn't care. The plush red velvet seats fascinated her, and the small rectangular windows beckoned her to look outside. The only thing in view was the flat, empty prairie, where she could look and look and look without seeing a thing. Five-year-old Mary, big as she was, begged to sit on Maudie's lap so she could gaze out the window, too.

The sun hung large and round in the west and darkness would soon fall. But Maudie was too tired to mind. After all the stress of moving, she was asleep when they left.

8

A New Name

GO, DANDY! GOOO!" Maudie shouted gleefully. Her little Shetland pony was nearly the same size as Giddley's, and they were almost a match.

"Go! Go! GO!" she prodded, kicking her bare legs against Dandy's sides. Dandy galloped hard to stay ahead of Daisy. Her broad, short hooves were pounding on the packed-dirt road.

Giddley lay low over Daisy's neck and held tightly to her thick blond mane. His legs squeezed her sides in a hard grip, and his eyes were mere slits.

He and Maudie bumped along on their short-legged ponies, both hoping to win the race. Staying almost neck and neck, the race was another close one. Daisy was ahead by only a nose, but just as the two children passed the corner post of their pasture, Dandy put on a final burst of speed and sailed ahead of her.

"Ohhh, that was fun!" Maudie shouted. The two ponies slowed to a trot and then a walk as they turned around.

"Uh, oh. Bess is crossing the road, Maudie," Giddley said breathlessly. "I'll go get her." And he kicked Daisy into another bumpy trot. They were herding the cows beside the road because there was lots of green grass growing there and the pasture in the field was getting thin. Giddley guided Daisy in front of Bessie and headed her back into the ditch, where she belonged. The other cows took short hurried bites, then walked ahead.

Since moving to Reno County, Father had bought Daisy and Dandy to help around the farm. They even pulled the family to church sometimes. But mostly they helped the children herd the cows beside the road. This was a daily chore, and Maudie and Giddley thoroughly enjoyed it.

It was spring and soon time to plant corn. The crop they harvested last year was more than enough to feed their turkeys, geese, and livestock, which numbered five more cows than they had brought from Ford County. Mother still raised chickens and sold the eggs for groceries and other household necessities.

Father had built an addition to the rundown barn, built a chicken house, and fixed up an old toolshed. The one-story house, with four bedrooms and a nice big kitchen, was in good condition and needed little work. But the farm had been sadly neglected and was in poor shape.

Father and the boys broke new soil and planted corn and oats. Rains fell nicely, and their first crop was plentiful—so different from their crops the past few years in Ford County. The soil was deep red and mellow, so they called it the Red Jaw place. Tall oak and elm trees shaded the house, and cottonwoods grew in the pasture. It was a nice home and Maudie loved it.

They had good neighbors, too. However, shortly after their arrival, Father thought they had chased away their neighbor to the east. Before he moved out, he had seemed rather strange. But Father befriended him, and soon the man stopped quite often to visit.

One day he began telling of their journey from New Mexico to Kansas. When he related how he had stopped in Ford County and milked a cow out in the pasture, Father began to smile knowingly.

"Was she right next to the railroad tracks?" Father asked.

"Why, yes," the man replied. "How do you know that?"

"Because that cow is out in the barnlot right now," Father said, his eyes twinkling merrily.

But the man saw no humor in the situation and soon left. He never returned again, and soon sold his farm and moved away. Father regretted having told him about Lady being the cow he had milked and that it was their oats he had stolen. If the man really needed that help, then Father would gladly have given it to him.

Time passed and Maudie was happy. She seldom thought of the home they left in Ford County, and when she did, she had only fond memories. Whenever she walked behind the toolshed and saw the big cast-iron wash kettle filled with rocks, broken hoe handles, and other worthless junk, she remembered Mose Troyer and his tricks. He had secretly put it on the train so Father would have to pay more for shipping. The old washpot hadn't amounted to much, as far as extra pounds were concerned, but it brought many a chuckle—even yet.

The only inconvenience here was the three-mile walk to school. But in time, Maudie did not mind even this. Kevin Whitt lived on the neighboring farm, and he and his sister Malinda walked to school with the Borntrager children. This helped to enliven the tiresome walk.

One crisp autumn morning, Maudie was late getting ready for school, so Mother told Giddley and Mary to go ahead. Taking Maudie by the arm, she marched her to the table and began unraveling Maudie's braids as fast as she could. Quickly she brushed her long, straight hair and braided them again. Maudie carelessly turned her head to see how far the other children had gone.

"Sit still, Maudie," Mother tapped her head sharply with the comb. But Maudie could hardly hold still.

Mother twisted the ends of her braids up and tied them with pink crochet threads. Then she wound them over the top of Maudie's head and fastened them with two hairpins. Finally Mother grabbed Maudie's covering, put it on her head, pinned it with straight pins, and tied the strings under her chin.

"Now go!" she said, helping her up and pushing her to the door.

"My bonnet!" Maudie cried as she felt the emptiness on her head.

"Here it is," Mother grabbed it off a hook on the wall and handed it to her. "And you'd better take your shawl, too, because it's pretty chilly this morning."

Maudie expertly swirled the shawl around her shoulders and

put the bonnet on her head without bothering to tie the strings. Then, grabbing her lunch pail, she rushed through the door and ran down the lane. As she neared the other children, she slowed to a fast walk. She did not want to be too out of breath when she got caught up with them.

As she followed, she saw Kevin stop at the little creek to throw stones into the water. He seemingly didn't care that the older children walked ahead. As Maudie neared him, she wondered what he was doing, all stooped over and staring into the water like that.

"What's the matter?" she asked.

"Oh, nothing," he replied. "I was just waiting on you."

"Oh?" Maudie's eyebrows shot up.

"Do you care if I walk with you?"

"*Vell* (Well)," she stammered. "I—I—guess not."

So the two walked to school together, although not much conversation passed between them. After school dismissed at three o'clock, Maudie hurried outside to start walking home before Kevin caught up with her again. But before long he was at her side, and they walked the three miles together.

That evening at the supper table, Giddley whispered to Jake, "Hey, Jake. Did you know Maudie has someone to walk to school with?"

Maudie kicked him under the table.

"Ouch!" he howled, dropping his fork to rub his leg.

"Children!" Mother reprimanded them in a no-nonsense tone of voice.

Maudie glared at Giddley, trying to make him be quiet. But he only grinned.

The next morning she asked Mary to walk with her so Kevin wouldn't. But when he and Malinda joined them, he fell in step beside her again. Inwardly, she liked it, but outwardly she pretended to be insulted. She hoped Mary would not tell Mother about it.

After school that afternoon, Kevin had to stay for a short while to help the teacher move her desk. Maudie wished he were with her. It seemed rather empty without him. She wondered if he would catch up with them or just walk behind. If he didn't want to walk with her anymore, she didn't blame him. After all, she hadn't treated him nicely. But soon he came running and fell in step next to her to walk home. This pleased her, for now she knew that he knew her true feelings.

One day at school she carefully wrote her name at the top of her slate: M a u d i e   B o r n t r a g e r. She looked critically at it and sighed. Such a plain name! Whoever wanted a Dutch name like that? Suddenly she didn't like her name at all. But because that was what Father and Mother had named her, then that was who she was—just plain old Maudie. That evening while walking home from school, she told Malinda that she didn't like her name.

"Why don't you change it?" Malinda asked.

"How can I do that?"

"Just decide what you want to be called and tell people to call you that." Malinda made anything sound simple.

Maudie thought about it all evening. She tried this name and that, but couldn't think of one that she really liked. And anyway, if she chose a name that was too fancy, like Victoria, Father wouldn't let her change her name. So she thought of all the Amish names she could. Finally she decided it would have to sound a lot like Maudie.

How about Mandie? she wondered. *Or Mattie.* Mattie was the Dutch name for Martha. She liked that. And the more she thought about it, the more she decided to write her name *Martha,* but ask people to call her *Mattie.* She wondered what people would think. But one thing was sure, she did not want to be Maudie the rest of her life.

The next morning she told Malinda that she had changed her name to Martha.

"But call me Mattie," she said. "That's the Dutch way to say it."

"Oh . . . I like that," Malinda smiled. "I knew you'd think of something nice . . . Mattie."

They burst out laughing.

"What's so funny?" Giddley asked. But the girls only looked at one another and giggled.

Kevin was searching their faces quizzically, and Maudie began to feel silly.

"She's not Maudie. She's *Mattie!*" Malinda told them emphatically.

Giddley's eyes opened wide and he exclaimed, "What?"

Gathering all her courage, Maudie took a deep breath and said, "I want to be called Mattie from now on. I don't like the name Maudie, and I think Mattie sounds nicer. But I really am Martha." A smile pulled at the corners of her mouth.

"Maarrthaaa," Giddley sneered in a singsong voice.

"Oh, stop it." Maudie swung her lunch pail at him.

Through all this, Mary had listened quietly. But now she spoke in Maudie's defense.

"I like that name, too, Giddley. And I don't think you ought to make fun of it."

"Yeah, I like it too," Kevin said.

So that settled it. Maudie was now Mattie and she told everyone to call her that. Now when she wrote her name on her slate, she did so with a great satisfaction: M a r t h a   B o r n t r a g e r. Mattie was growing up and she liked it.

When the spring winds begin to blow after the long, hard winter, Mother became anxious to plant her garden. She had carefully saved seeds from the previous year and stored them in small tins in the pantry. Each tin was neatly labeled, and Mother knew exactly how she wanted her garden arranged.

The potatoes must be planted in the outside rows so they could be dug without uprooting other tender plants. A separate garden plot was planted behind the barn for the melons. Early in the spring she planted potatoes, English peas, carrots, and red beets.

Planting the early garden was something the children anticipated. The soft mellow soil sifted between their toes and tickled their tender feet. Sometimes they planted the garden just before a rain, trying desperately to finish before it fell. Other times the skies were crystal clear, with a high sun shining warmly on their backs. Such was the weather in April 1915.

Mary sat on the ground at the edge of the garden cutting potatoes for planting. With a paring knife she carefully cut each potato into several pieces, making sure each piece had an eye in it. The sprouts grew from these eyes. Mattie and Giddley dropped the chunks of potatoes into the holes Mother dug, and Sarah followed with a pail of water and poured a small glassful over each one. Then she went back and covered them up, pouring another glassful over the top.

The mockingbirds perched on top of the windmill and made music. Then they swooped high in the sky, gently floating and dipping before settling back on the blades of the windmill. Mattie thought they sang the prettiest songs. Sometimes it was "Tobe-e-e. Tobe-e-e. Tobe-e-e." Then they warbled, "Pretty girl, pretty girl." Sometimes their songs were only for birds to understand, like "Cheee, cheee, chee."

While Mattie paused to watch the birds, she suddenly saw something in the southwestern sky that puzzled her. It was a large buzzing . . . something! What was it?

Giddley saw it almost at the same time, pointed toward it, and shouted, "Oh, look!" Steadily it droned toward them. Then they saw wings and a thick body in the center of it.

"It's an airplane," Mother told them.

"But why doesn't it fall down?" Giddley asked.

"I don't know," Mother whispered, her eyes never leaving the approaching plane.

The motor grew louder and louder, making the chickens squawk and run for the chicken house. The cows threw up their tails and jumped and ran about, too confused to find shelter. Cap and Dolly and the two Shetlands, Dandy and Daisy, snorted and ran pell-mell for the far side of the pasture. But when they reached it, they wheeled about, throwing up dirt and racing along the fence going back the way they had come.

Lydia, who had been playing quietly beneath the elm tree, began crying hysterically. "Mama! Mama! Mama!" she screamed. Mother ran to pick her up.

"It's an airplane, Lydia," she told her. "See? It won't hurt you."

Now they could see the propeller on the front and the pilot in the cockpit. Giddley waved, and to their delight and astonishment, the airplane dipped its wings up and down.

Mattie wished it had passed directly over them instead of over the pasture. But even so, it was close enough for them to see it plainly. How such a large machine could stay in the air without falling down was a mystery to her. What would people invent next?

9

The Sticky Mess

MATTIE LOOKED OUT the-living room window and watched a strange buggy driving in their lane.

"Who's coming?" Mary asked.

"I don't know," Mattie replied. Then suddenly she recognized the driver to be Jonas Yoder. His wife, who was expecting a baby, probably needed a maid to help with the housework. Sarah was helping another new mother and wouldn't come home until Friday. A feeling of dread stole over Mattie.

"Mother, Jonas is here!" Mary shouted.

"Be quiet, Mary!" Mattie whispered loudly to her sister. "He's going to hear you yet."

Mother bustled into the living room, wiping her hands on her apron.

"He wants a maid, I'm sure," Mother said. "And Sarah's over at Levi's. Well, well, well."

Jonas opened the gate and walked to the house and up the steps to the front door. Mother opened it before he had time to knock.

"Come in, Jonas," she invited him.

"No, that's okay, Mary. Edna had the baby last night, and we need a maid to come help. We thought of your Sarah and would really like to have her if we can."

"Well . . . Sarah is helping Levi's right now, so she can't come." Mother looked thoughtful. "But Mattie is here and I think she could handle it."

Mattie had helped neighbors before, but never longer than a

day at a time. More than likely this would be for a week or maybe two. But there was no point in arguing. If Mother knew of someone who needed help, she would not turn them away, even if it meant going herself.

Mother and Jonas were looking expectantly at her, so Mattie carefully hid her feelings.

"Go get your things together, Mattie," Mother instructed her.

There was nothing she could do but go to her bedroom, gather her clothes, and go along.

The Jonas Yoder home was neat and orderly. Their two older children looked as though they were freshly bathed. Mattie was shown the room she would share with the two girls, Lena and Beth, and numbly hung her dresses in the small closet.

Then she went to the kitchen, unsure of what to do. Jonas came out of the bedroom and told her that Edna said she could begin preparing their supper.

"What shall I make?" she asked in a thin voice.

"Oh, I don't know. Let me ask Edna." He disappeared into their bedroom again and seemed to be gone for a long time. When he returned, he told Mattie to make hamburger gravy and rice.

"Hamburger gravy and rice!" Mattie thought in astonishment. Both dishes were something the Borntragers seldom had. The gravy, no doubt, would not be as hard. But the rice—she had no idea how to make rice! She walked to the cupboard, lifted two kettles down, and set them on the cabinet beside the stove. Turning to the two little girls, who were standing stiffly beside the table, she asked where to find the hamburger.

"Out there in the cellar," Lena pointed to the backyard.

Mattie walked outside and looked around for the cellar door. A small rooftop could be seen in the yard. She lifted the door on the end and descended into its dark, damp interior. When her eyes adjusted to the dim light, she saw row upon row of canned goods neatly arranged in groups according to the variety of fruits, meats, or vegetables. Edna was particular, Mattie soon realized, and it did nothing for her self-confidence.

She soon found the meats, took a jar of hamburger from the shelf, and turned to go back to the house. Suddenly she noticed that all the jars were sitting on the edges of the shelves. None were part way back, as though a jar had been taken from the front. So Mattie went back and pulled the next jar forward until it, too, stood at the edge of the shelf.

Deep within, a growing feeling of despair threatened to choke her. With great apprehension, she walked back to the house, where she knew the little girls would be watching every move she made. And probably Edna would be listening to make sure she was doing things properly.

She opened the jar of hamburger and scraped it into the frying pan. Then with a large wooden spoon, she broke the meat apart, poured milk over it, and put a lid on top. Taking the rice from a shelf, she poured some into a kettle and covered it with water. She asked the girls if they knew how to set the table. They silently nodded their heads and began taking dishes from the cupboard.

At least they have been taught how to work, Mattie thought. She wondered if she should prepare something else to go with the rice. Just hamburger didn't seem like enough. Jonas was a big man and he would be hungry. She remembered seeing green beans in the cellar, so she hurried back outside and descended the cellar steps. This time she knew where to look and soon had the jar of beans in her hand. She remembered to pull the next jar forward to sit on the edge of the shelf.

When she returned to the kitchen, a strange odor greeted her. In horror she lifted the lid on the hamburger, but to her relief discovered it just beginning to boil. Then she lifted the lid on the rice. She wondered if she had done something wrong. It looked alright, but the smell made her wonder. She took a spoon from a drawer and tried to stir it, but encountered a hard, sticky mass.

It must need more water, she decided. Feverishly, she grabbed the pitcher of water and poured some into the kettle. Stirring it brought little improvement. She poured in more water and stirred. This time the grains of rice began to separate and stir easier.

Mattie covered the kettle of rice and returned to the hamburger. It looked like it was time to add the thickening. She tried hard to remember how Mother made thickenings for gravy and recalled seeing her shake flour and milk together in a little jar. There was no empty jar in the kitchen, so she ran to the cellar again, knowing there were some there. She grabbed one off a shelf and looked helplessly about for lids. Not finding them, she decided to send one of the little girls out to get one.

This time when she returned to the kitchen, the smell of burning rice sent sharp stabs of fear into her heart. When she lifted the lid off the kettle, a great cloud of white smoke billowed to the ceiling. She snatched a hot pad, pulled the kettle off the stove, and rushed to the sink. Then she grabbed another kettle from the cupboard and quickly dumped the rice into it, being careful not to transfer the burned rice from the bottom of the hot kettle. Her hands were shaking and her cheeks burned.

Suddenly she remembered the hamburger. It had been boiling when she went outside. Soon it would be burning, too. Leaving the kettle of rice in the sink, she hurried to the stove and lifted the lid on the hamburger. It had nearly boiled dry, so Mattie quickly added more milk. Now she would have a little more time to take care of the rice until the fresh milk began to boil. She poured more water from the pitcher into the rice and set it back on the stove. Then she remembered to send one of the girls to the cellar to get a lid for the jar.

"There are lids right here," Lena said as she pulled a drawer out beside the stove.

There, in a neat row, were several pint jars with lids lying loosely on top.

"Oh, okay. I wouldn't have needed to go to the cellar after this other one then," Mattie remarked, feeling a little foolish. Lena only stared at her. Mattie knew that she must be wondering why she was doing things the way she was.

She poured some milk into the jar and added flour to it. Mother had often done it like that. She screwed the lid down tight and shook it vigorously.

Soon she began to smell the rice again. She set the jar of thickening on the back of the stove and lifted the lid over the rice once more. To her surprise, all the water had dried up and it needed more. The kettle was nearly full of rice, and Mattie wondered if she would need to put it into a bigger kettle. She poured all the water from the pitcher into the kettle and hoped she would not need anymore. If she did, she'd have to go out to the pump after it.

Now she turned to the gravy, lifted the lid, and with the wooden spoon began to stir the thickening into it. At least she felt she was doing this right. The milk stopped bubbling as she stirred and soon began getting thick and lumpy. Gradually it began to boil again, and the longer it boiled, the thicker it became. Mattie added more milk and continued to stir. But the lumps would not go away, and as it returned to the boiling point again, it grew thick and pasty.

Mattie stirred in more milk. Then she checked the rice. It had risen to the very top of the kettle, and Mattie thought it was probably ready. Taking a fork, she stirred a few grains at the top and thought they looked dry and fluffy, like they were supposed to. With a great sigh of relief, she lifted the kettle from the stove and set it in the sink. When she turned back to the gravy, she saw she would again need to stir in more milk. Just then the back door opened and Jonas appeared.

"Suppertime?" he asked good-naturedly.

Mattie wiped the sweat from her forehead and nodded. Suddenly she remembered the beans she had planned to heat. Hurriedly, she dumped them into the last kettle in the cupboard and placed them on the stove. Then she poured the last of the milk into the gravy and stirred briskly, hoping the lumps would disappear. But instead, they only seemed thicker and more pasty than before.

"Lena and Beth, you can pour the water for Mattie," Jonas

prompted the confused little girls. "And put the bread and butter on, too."

Mattie had forgotten about the bread and butter and was glad he remembered them. She opened the cupboard doors in search of serving bowls. Taking two of the largest, she set them on the cabinet and poured gravy into one and rice into the other. Even after filling them to the top, she only half-emptied the kettles. *What will I do with all the leftovers?* she wondered.

She carried the bowls to the table and returned for the beans. At least she didn't make twice too many of them. She emptied them into a serving bowl and, in a shy and embarrassed tone of voice, told Jonas that supper was ready. Her knees were shaking as she sat down to the table, and while she waited for Jonas and the girls to sit down, her eyes swept over the kitchen in dismay. What a mess! She hoped they wouldn't notice.

After bowing their heads in silent prayer, Mattie began spooning out food for the girls. Jonas prepared a plate for Edna and took it to her. Mattie hoped the rice would not taste burnt. No one mentioned it, but she felt sure they thought about it. The gravy didn't taste too bad, although it certainly was not like Mother's.

She ate in silence, too embarrassed to speak. One thing was certain: she knew they would never ask her to make rice and gravy again. And maybe, just maybe, she would make it through the week.

By Friday, Mattie was nearly bursting to go home. How she longed for the carefree days when she and Giddley raced Daisy and Dandy beside the road. And she hoped Sarah would be at home for the weekend. Now they had something in common, and she couldn't wait to talk with her about it. When Jonas took her home, he handed her two dollars for the week's pay. Never before had Mattie been paid for something, and it made her feel important.

Sarah did indeed come home, and a restful weekend it was. Tobe was dating Nettie Knepp, and the children teased him unmercifully. Mattie believed Sarah had her eye on someone, too, but Sarah denied it.

Giddley, especially, loved to tease. He would never in his whole life get married to a silly old girl, he claimed. And to see Tobe fall so hard for Nettie was a big joke to him. Daisy was his girlfriend, and he would never need another one.

But one day when Mattie and Giddley were racing Daisy and Dandy full speed through the pasture, Daisy suddenly took a stubborn notion and stopped unexpectedly. Giddley flew fast and hard over Daisy's head and landed in a heap in front of her. He lay so still that Mattie began wondering if he had been knocked unconscious. But he slowly got to his feet, brushed the dust from his pants, and rubbed the bruised spots on his back and neck.

Never again did Giddley proclaim the virtues of Daisy. And never again did he race with Mattie.

Soon Mattie was working for other people more than at home. She worked hard and tried her best to please her employers. But always there was a deep longing in her heart to stay at home with Mother and Mary and Lydia. She wished Sarah would not have to work away as often either.

It seemed as though her family was gradually growing apart as they saw less and less of each other. She supposed Tobe was thinking of getting married before too long. Then their family would forever be different.

Mattie felt sad at the changes. Is this how it felt to grow up? Was the world of grownups not as pleasant as she had always supposed? Sometimes Mattie just wanted to stay small—like right now.

10

Wedding Day

MATTIE STRAIGHTENED her back and shifted her position on the hard bench. The minister's voice droned on and on and Mattie wondered when the service would end. Tobe and Nettie sat perfectly still on chairs in the front of the room, and Mattie wondered what they were thinking.

A wedding was exciting, and Mattie couldn't help envying Nettie just a little. She wouldn't want to get married now, but someday she hoped to. Then she would not have to work for other women. Instead, she would have her own house to keep.

She could do as she pleased, get up when she wanted, and take a nap in the afternoon. If she wanted to sit down and rock her baby—why, then she could. And she would have a husband who cared for her and, well . . . she was sure she would be very happy.

She looked out the window where the morning sun played among the leaves of the oak trees. They were turning brown, and the maple trees were taking on rich red and golden hues. The cornfields were ready to shock, and Mattie knew that the next week would be a busy one, with the wedding behind them now.

Ordinarily September meant school, but now that Mattie was fifteen years old, her school days were over. Never again would she sit in a warm classroom with autumn breezes stirring the pages of her books. Now her days were mostly spent working for mothers of new babies, and seldom was she allowed to stay at home. Unless, of course, they had to get ready for a wedding. Tobe was marrying today, and if all went as she suspected, Sarah would soon follow.

She turned her attention back to the ceremony. Suddenly her eyes met those of Nettie's younger brother, Sam. He looked about to be thirteen or fourteen years old, with light blond hair and startlingly blue eyes. His hair was cut in true Dutchboy fashion: straight across his forehead, down in front of his ears, and then straight around the back of his neck. She had never seen a haircut quite like it and thought it looked strange.

But his eyes struck her. Were they serious or laughing? She couldn't be sure. She didn't want to look at him too much or he might think she had a fancy for him. Still, there was something about him that attracted her.

At long last the minister finished speaking and the congregation knelt to pray. When the prayer was over, Tobe and Nettie rose and stood side by side before the bishop to say their vows: "Till death do us part."

Another prayer was prayed and a song sung before the ceremony was over and Mattie could stand and stretch her legs and ease her aching back. Three buggies waited in front of the house to take Tobe and Nettie and the bridal party to her home. There a bountiful meal would be served. The ceremony had been held at the neighbor's so Nettie's home could be prepared for the dinner.

The mothers and aunts and the *hustlers* (waiters) had not attended the ceremony. Instead, they worked feverishly to get the tables and food ready. Most of the food had been prepared the day before, but there was still a lot of work involved in getting everything ready for the guests by twelve o'clock.

After Tobe and Nettie and their attendants hurried to the waiting buggies, the rest of the congregation moved slowly out the front door. A long line of slow-moving buggies wound its way out of the neighbor's driveway and to the Knepp home.

Buggies were tied all along the fence from the road to the Knepp barn and even behind the barn. And still more buggies came. Mattie, Giddle (who thought he was too old to be called Giddley now), Mary, and Lydia patiently waited for their turn to get into line.

"It would be faster to walk," Giddle observed as he idly fingered the reins in his hands. Other boys were walking along the road, and now and then there was a group of young girls.

When they eventually reached the Knepp home, there was no room for their buggy in the yard, so they tied Dolly to the fence by the road. Nettie's brother Sam was standing on the porch watching the guests arrive. When he saw Mattie and Giddle walking toward him, he turned self-consciously away. Mattie felt uncomfortable, too, as they stepped up to the porch and waited until they could enter the living room.

Once inside, they were allowed to sit at a table in the far corner of the room because they were of Tobe's family. Others had to sit in a back room or wait until the first ones were finished eating.

Tobe and Nettie and the attendants sat at the *Eck* (corner) of a large table. A simple cake was the only decoration. Nettie sat on one side of the *Eck,* while Tobe sat on the other, with the witnesses on either side.

The *hustlers,* Sarah, Dan, Jake, Nettie's brothers and sisters, and some other young people, brought bowls of chicken, noodles, potatoes, gravy, corn, beans, and peas. There were several salads, pickled red beets, and cucumbers. For dessert there was angel food cake, and pies, pies, pies. Cherry and apple and coconut and chocolate. Everything was delicious. As soon as she, Giddle, Mary, and Lydia finished eating, they left the table so others could sit down.

As the afternoon passed and people finished their dinner, families began to leave. There were chores to be done and children to put to bed. But the young people stayed for an evening of singing and supper.

Even Mattie was allowed to stay, although she was not yet sixteen, the official age to attend the youth gatherings. She felt shy and out of place but yet wanted to stay. Tobe and Nettie sat together in the front of the room and led the first song.

The sun sank in the west in a riot of colors, and the air began to cool as darkness gathered around them. Lamps were lit and

Mattie noticed Katie, Nettie's mother, sink in exhaustion onto the only chair available. She admired her serenity in spite of the day's stressful activities.

Nettie came from a good home, she was sure. Even though her father, Levi, had only one arm, nothing slowed him down. He had apparently taught his family how to work and to enjoy it.

Mattie thought Sam resembled his father and that his quiet manner belied the industrious way he had done the evening chores. She had watched him begin the milking without being told and saw how he hurried about the farmyard, gathering the eggs and slopping the hog. *If only he would cut his hair differently*, she thought.

They sang and sang until Mattie began to tire of it. She went outside to refresh herself for a few minutes and was surprised to discover more young people on the porch steps and leaning on the railing, quietly talking and laughing. Mattie stood just outside the door and listened to their conversation.

When her eyes had adjusted to the darkness, she saw Sarah sitting on the top step of the porch. She moved timidly to her and sat down. After listening quietly for some time, Sarah turned to Mattie and said, "So Tobe's married now."

"Yep," Mattie replied. "Next it'll be you."

Sarah smiled in spite of herself, even though she insisted it would be a long time before she married. "Dan and Polly will get married before Ammon and I do."

"Oh, I wouldn't be so sure about that," Mattie said.

Suddenly, she became aware of someone standing next to them and looked up to see Anna Bontrager. She moved over to make room for her.

"They're almost ready to eat now," Anna told them, looking through the windows at the table laden with food. Then she dropped her voice and leaned closer to Mattie, as though to tell her a secret. "Jacob wants to know if you'd sit with him for supper."

Mattie looked at Anna in surprise. "Me?"

"Yes. He told me to ask you."

"But I'm not sixteen yet."

"Well . . . it's not really a date."

Mattie looked out into the night and pondered over her predicament. *What would Father say?* He had told the children they could not date until they were sixteen. And she would not have her sixteenth birthday for another month.

Sarah had heard the conversation and smiled knowingly. "Jacob?" she asked.

Mattie nodded her head.

"Are you going to sit with him?"

"I'm not sixteen yet, so I don't think I should," Mattie decided. Then turning to Anna, she told her to tell Jacob that she wasn't old enough.

"Aw, come on," Anna encouraged her. But Mattie's mind was made up, and she insisted that she was not going to do things like that until she was sixteen. So Anna rose from the porch steps and returned to the living room.

Everyone had stopped singing, and some of the boys were jostling and teasing each other to ask various girls to sit with them during the supper. The dating couples went to the table and sat down, with Tobe and Nettie on the end. The girls who had no steady boyfriends pretended to be reluctant to sit with a boy when asked or were actually too shy to do so.

Finally, some of the boys went to the kitchen and grabbed tea towels. They wrapped them tightly and snapped them at the girls to make them go to the table. So with much screaming and laughter, everyone was finally seated. Mattie sat with Nettie's younger sister and brother, Cora and Sam, at the far end of the table.

Finally all were quiet enough to pray, but as they bowed their heads, Mattie was keenly aware of Sam across the table from her. They ate in silence, content to listen to the older young people teasing and joking with each other. Mattie wasn't hungry because of the large dinner at noon, but she ate a piece of chicken and a sumptuous piece of chocolate pie.

She noticed that Sam ate two pieces of coconut pie and decided that it must be his favorite. Occasionally their eyes met and each time they both looked away, embarrassed. Mattie was relieved when the meal was over at last and it was time to go home. It wasn't that she didn't enjoy being with the young people, but she just didn't feel like she belonged.

While riding home with Dan, Jake, and Sarah, she looked across the darkened countryside and rehearsed the events of the day. Nettie had been so beautiful in her soft blue woolen dress. And Tobe had stood straight and tall beside her while saying their vows. She thought there was no one in the world as handsome as he.

"I guess Tobe won't be going with us anymore, will he?" Jake remarked.

"Nope," Dan shook his head.

Mattie knew they, too, were thinking about how much their family was changing. Times would never be the same.

"I think Tobe has a good wife, though," Jake added.

"Yeah, I like Nettie," Sarah agreed.

"I do too," Mattie nodded.

They rode in silence for several miles and listened to the night sounds. It was well past midnight and no lights burned anywhere. All was very dark, with only the stars sparkling in the sky.

"Why didn't you sit with Jacob tonight, Mattie?" Dan asked.

"Because Father told us we can't date until we're sixteen, and I'm not sixteen yet."

"But it wouldn't have been a date—just sitting with him during supper."

"I don't care," Mattie insisted.

She didn't feel comfortable with boys yet and was determined to wait to date until she was sixteen. Besides, what did it matter? Her time would come.

11

Lazybones!

MATTIE WISHED IT WERE only a dream. A dream from which she would awake in the pearly good morning and know that all was well. But it was no dream. And all was not well.

It was no dream that their beautiful home was sold. And it was no dream that Jake was in New Mexico, possibly dying of pneumonia. And it was no dream that she, Mary, and Giddle were moving the last of their belongings to New Mexico by train.

Tobe and Nettie, who were now married for several years, had two children. They, along with Dan and his new wife, Polly, and Jake and Father had moved to New Mexico several months earlier. Tobe's youngest child, two-year-old Crist, had been too sick to go along then. So they decided he would travel with Mother later.

But then, plans changed. Jake became deathly ill with pneumonia, and Mother had to leave immediately to care for him. She had taken Lydia with her. This had left most of the work and responsibility upon Mattie, and she had not wanted to leave their home in Kansas in the first place.

Sarah was married, too, and she and Ammon were staying in Kansas. So it had been doubly hard to leave, not knowing when they would see Sarah again.

Word had spread of the inexpensive land that could be bought in New Mexico and the bountiful crops being harvested there. Tobe, Dan, Jake, and Father were immediately interested and traveled there to investigate. They returned full of excitement and plans.

Father sold their home and eighty acres. With that money he completely paid for a whole section of virgin prairie—a whopping 640 acres. Of course, it was not cultivated or fenced and had no buildings on it. But Father was a carpenter, so this posed no problem for him. He would soon have houses built.

Father firmly believed that the move there would be the best for his family. Mother had grave doubts but bravely hoped Father was right. And Mattie, Mary, and Lydia also had doubts. But Father and the boys were absolutely certain all would be well in New Mexico.

When Mattie, Giddle, Mary, and little Crist arrived in Springer, New Mexico, Father was waiting with a new horse and wagon. It had been a long and tiresome journey, especially for little Crist. Keeping the active toddler entertained had been no easy task.

Now Crist leaped into his grandfather's arms. With a loud whoop, Mattie's father snatched him up and threw him high into the air, then caught him again. Crist giggled happily, and that joy banished the tiredness Mattie had felt only a short hour before. It was so good to see Father.

"How's Jake?" Mary asked, almost before Father had time to catch his breath.

Father swung Crist onto his shoulders and let a deep sigh escape his lips before answering. "He's doing better. We feel sure he'll make it now, but he's pretty weak. It will take a while for him to really get over this."

His eyes were somber, and Mattie realized in a new way how serious Jake's illness had been. "It's a good thing Mother came when she did," he added.

He set Crist down on the wide platform so he could help get their things out of the boxcar. Crist wanted to run in wide circles, but Mattie hung onto him. There were too many people around for monkeyshines.

Finally the last of their boxes and crates were loaded on the wagon and they began the thirty-mile trek to their home. Mattie couldn't help staring at the awesome landscape they intended to call home.

"Is this a place to live?" she murmured.

"That's what I'd like to know," Mary said quietly.

"Of course it's a place to live!" Father exclaimed in his loud, booming voice. "Isn't it Crist?" he squeezed his trusting grandson nestled in his lap. Crist giggled and nodded happily.

All around to the south and east was flat, barren prairie, without a landmark in sight. To the far, far west were mountains stretching as far as they could see. And to the north was a curious looking mountain that rose straight up and was long and flat on top. Just to the east of it and a little farther north was another one that reminded Mattie of an elephant with his feet stuck in the ground.

"Look at that mountain over there, Giddle. It looks like an elephant."

The shape of an elephant's head and trunk were clearly visible.

"It's called Elephant's Peak," Father told them. "And the other one you see that's long and flat is called Hog Back." He pointed back toward Elephant's Peak and asked if they could see the strange-looking one that was a little behind and to the east of it. It resembled a straw stack with several smaller straw stacks clustered around it. "That's called the Seven Sisters."

The prairie was wild and empty. Except for the distant mountains, there was nothing to be seen—no houses, no trees, not even a fence post. There was no sign of life anywhere, and Mattie began to wonder if they were the only living beings on the entire earth.

"How do you know which way to go to get to our place?" she asked Father.

"I just follow my nose," he answered.

"But how does your nose know which way to go?"

"It's been this way before."

Mattie could only wonder and hope that Father would not get lost. The sun was setting in breathtaking, fiery colors, more beautiful than Mattie had even seen. Wispy clouds flung thin wings carelessly up and outward as though to take all the room in the great wide sky. Mattie looked up and up and up. The sky seemed so much larger than it had in Reno County, Kansas, even larger than what she remembered it was in Ford County. The air was dry and hot.

Tiny stars peeked through the gathering dusk and shone straight at her. They did not twinkle by the wayside as they did in Kansas, but shone steady and clear. Suddenly she noticed a thin slice of the silvery moon suspended above the setting sun.

"At least they have the same moon here," she mumbled to herself.

Several hours later they arrived at a small adobe house. It was squatty and dingy. Mattie wondered who lived there. It did not occur to her that this was home.

"This is Dan's house, but we're living here too until we get our house built," Father informed them.

Mattie was shocked! She knew life would not be as it had been in Kansas, but she had expected more than this. The girls spent the night on the hard dirt floor, just inside the door. It was warm and humid with too many bodies in too-tight quarters.

Mattie dozed fitfully, never quite relaxing. Suddenly, she sat bolt upright. Almost at the same time, Mary sat up too.

"What was that?" Mary whispered hoarsely.

"I don't know."

Something had awakened them, but neither knew what it had been. Suddenly sharp yipping sounds filled the night air and chills ran up their spines. The yips seemed to circle the small house and tremble through the open window, rising and falling and rising again, and then suddenly all was quiet. Mattie and Mary stared wide-eyed into the darkness.

"What can it be?" Mary whispered.

"I don't know. But it must not be too serious or the others would hear it too."

"Should we wake Mother?"

"No. She's tired and it's probably nothing that will get us."

Mary argued that it might be something dangerous. But after listening for a long time and hearing nothing more, she finally lay down again. The next time they heard the high yipping sounds, they came from much further away. Mattie was reassured that, whatever was yipping, it was not dangerous. In a way, it was nice to know that they were not the only living beings in the world, even if the others were wild animals.

The next morning dawned with a bright hot sun bearing down on them. The prairie looked different in the daylight. The grasses were taller and the house seemed larger.

Mattie was startled to see Jake, thin and pale, on the couch. He lay with eyes closed, and she wasn't sure if he was asleep or awake. But when he heard her taking up the quilts, he opened his eyes and smiled.

"Welcome home," he gestured with a weak wave of his hand.

"Home?" Mattie asked. "Is this a place to live?"

"Of course it's a place to live."

"Well, it sure isn't home like we're used to."

"Give us time."

"How do you feel?"

"I just need a little rest, and then I'll be all right again.," He raised himself onto his elbow and smoothed the quilt with his free hand.

Mary and Lydia were awake and began chattering as though they hadn't seen each other for a year.

"Hey!" Mattie suddenly remembered. "Mary and I heard the scariest noise last night. It sounded like wolves or something."

"Oh, yeah," Lydia said. "Did they go like this . . . yip, yip, yip, yiiiippppp?" Her voice quavered in perfect imitation of the wild voices they had heard.

"Yesssss!" Mary answered. "Just like that! What were they?"

"Coyotes."

"Didn't they scare you the first time you heard them?"

"Naw. I was a brave little girl."

"Oh, you were not!" Mary pushed her shoulder.

"She probably climbed into bed with Mother," Mattie added.

"No, I didn't. I just covered up my head and lay real still. I didn't wake anybody."

"How would you like to be out on the open prairie like I was, with nothing between you and them but a wagon and a little old campfire?" Jake asked.

"You probably shinnied up inside the wagon when you heard them," Mary teased him.

"No, I didn't. I just covered up my head, too, and wished they would go away."

"My, but you were a brave little boy." Mary clicked her tongue.

It was so good to be together again that Mattie didn't mind the close quarters and this seemingly God-forsaken country. Mother and Polly asked them to come and eat breakfast, so the girls hurriedly folded the quilts and piled them in a corner.

"Where do Tobe and Nettie live?" Mattie asked.

"Over that way on the neighbor's land." Father pointed to the east. "They're renting a house there."

"You mean there are houses around here?" she asked.

"Of course," he answered. "We're not the only people on this land."

"Well, you couldn't tell it by looking."

"Oh, Mattie, it's not that bad," Dan chuckled. "There's a lot more going on around here than coyotes howling."

They laughed and all too soon breakfast was over and it was time to get to work. There was so much work to be done that they hardly knew where to begin. Father had built Dan and Polly's house since arriving and dug a hole in the ground for theirs. Now he was ready to begin on the top part.

Building into the ground helped to keep the house cool in the summer and warm in the winter. Adobe blocks would be laid for walls and then the roof was made of lumber overlaid with a thick layer of sod. Mattie wondered how it would be done but did not have long to wait to find out.

"You girls come on out to the buffalo hollow as soon as you're done with your work here in the house," Father instructed them.

"Giddle, hitch Nellie up to the disk and bring her out."

Mattie, Mary, and Lydia hurriedly washed the dishes and

straightened the kitchen. Although it was small and had only one window on the west end, Polly had whitewashed the walls, and it was bright and cheery.

The buffalo hollow was a place in the prairie where buffalo had dug a hole in the sod and water had collected. When the girls arrived, they found Father hard at work driving Nellie and the disk through the water. Father had cut prairie grasses and hauled them to the hollow. Now he made a thick grassy mud. He plodded back and forth and back and forth until he was satisfied it was of the right consistency.

Lydia showed her sisters the wooden molds Father had made. They were a foot square and six inches deep. She soaked them in the water tank, then piled them into the wheelbarrow to take back to the hollow. There she showed them how to pack the forms hard and tight and lay them in the sun to dry.

When they had dried only a little, just enough to hold their shape, she dumped the block out onto the grassy slope. There the blocks would dry for several days until they were as hard as rock. These were top-quality adobe blocks, the best material around from which to build a house.

All the long day Mattie, Mary, and Lydia soaked the molds, carried them back to the hollow, filled and packed them with the thick grassy mud, and then dumped them out onto the grassy slope. The sun beat down mercilessly, but still they worked. By evening their hands were rough and sore and their faces burned from the hot sun. But it would be worth all the work just to have a nice house of their own.

Several days later Father began the actual building of the house. He would need a minimum amount of lumber, so Tobe, Dan, Giddle, and two neighbor boys, Harry and Ezra, left early one morning, long before sunrise. It was a long day's journey by horse and wagon to the mountains, where there was a lumber mill. They would need to spend the night there and come home the next day, not arriving until long after dark.

Mattie felt uneasy about their going, but she knew they really had no other choice. Lumber was scarce and they were fortunate to live close enough to the mountains to be able to get it.

After breakfast Father had another job for the girls to do. There was a beautiful plant growing on the prairie with fernlike leaves and lovely purple and yellow flowers. But alas! it was the locoweed, a poisonous plant. Cows and horses loved it but could quickly eat enough of it to destroy their minds.

So Mattie, Mary, and Lydia took shovels and the wheelbarrow and walked far and wide over the prairie, digging up the beautiful locoweeds and piling them on the ground. In the evening they burned them there. It was almost hard to imagine that something so beautiful could be so dangerous.

At sunset when they walked past their new house, they saw that Father was nearly finished with the outside walls. It looked small in comparison to the large two-story house he had built in Kansas. Because the floor of the house was dug into the ground several feet, the walls were only about five feet high on the outside.

There was one window on the west end and a door on the east end. There would be three bedrooms, one for the three girls, one for Giddle and Jake, and one for Mother and Father. Then there would be a big room that would serve as kitchen, dining room, and living room. All looked dark and drab now, but the girls hoped it would look nicer once they had their furniture in and the walls whitewashed as Polly had.

They walked on to Dan's house to begin the evening chores and help Mother and Polly get supper. Jake was sitting outside with his chair leaning back against the house. As they approached, he began lazily whistling a tune.

"Listen to him!" Lydia scoffed.

"Hey, Lazybones! What have you been doing all day?" Mary called to him.

He didn't bother to answer but continued whistling and watching the sunset.

"Lazybones!" Mattie called. "Hey, Lazybones!"

Still he did not answer.

The three sisters decided to call to him together.

"LAAZZYYBONNNESSS!!!!"

By now they were standing directly in front of him, their hands cupped over their mouths. Bending down, they looked into his twinkling eyes.

"Did you say something?" he asked innocently.

"Yes! We'd like to talk with Lazybones," Mattie yelled.

"He's not here."

"Yes, he is," they said in unison.

"Don't you do anything besides nothing all day?" Mary chided him.

"No, I did nothing besides nothing all day today. Do you want to trade places?"

"Of course!" Mary said. She grabbed him by the arm and tried to pull him out of his chair. "I'd like to sit here and whistle all day, everyday for once and do nothing besides nothing."

"Go ahead." Jake stood up to give her his chair. "We'll see how long you can sit there and do nothing."

She leaned her head back against the rough adobe blocks and began whistling a lively tune.

"Go, get us chairs, Jake. That looks like fun," Mattie told him.

"Get your own chairs if it's so much fun," he replied.

She gave him a playful kick, and he returned it. Then she shoved him toward the door. He pushed her back hard and nearly threw her over.

"*Unleidlich!* (Unbearable!)" she said. "I think if you are that strong, then you can dig up locoweed and we girls can sit here in the shade and watch you."

"So that's what's wrong with you girls tonight. You've had too much of the locoweed!" he replied, sounding as though he had discovered a gold mine.

They looked at each other and burst out laughing. "Yeah, we've had too much locoweed."

After supper they pulled chairs outside to sit in the cool breeze until bedtime.

"I bet you wish you could have gone with the other boys," Mattie said to Jake sympathetically.

"I sure do," he answered.

"I don't," she said.

"You don't what?"

"I don't wish you were with them. And I'm glad I'm not with them either."

"You're scared of the wolves."

"Not really. But you never know who or what you'll meet in this wild country on a night like this, with no moon and all. Even the stars aren't out tonight."

"What difference does that make?"

"I don't know." After a few minutes she added, "I'm just glad I'm here and not there."

"I think it would be fun to go up in the mountains and camp like the cowboys."

"Not me! I'm not a cowboy and I'm not a cowgirl. I'm just a plain Amish girl that likes to stay at home."

"They should be coming home before too long." Jake looked toward the mountains in the north. There was only a smudge of blackness on the horizon. Their conversation turned to other things, and Dan, Tobe, and Giddle were soon forgotten.

Suddenly they heard a strange noise coming from the north. It was a drumming sound, like many horses running. And a creaking and squealing like a wooden wagon being pulled too fast. They jumped up and strained to see what it could be.

As the noise drew closer, they saw the dim shapes of two horses approaching at breakneck speed. Another horse and wagon was rumbling and careening across the prairie behind them, dust flying and lumber bouncing.

Two horses with Giddle and Tobe riding low over their necks galloped into the yard and whirled to a stop in front of the makeshift barn. Then the wagon came thundering into the yard, and Dan and the neighbor boys, Ezra and Harry, jumped off it and ran to the house. Not stopping to tie the horses or to explain, they pushed past the girls and Jake and burst through the door. They stood against the stove, breathing hard and trembling.

"Boys!' Mother exclaimed.

"It's wolves!" they shouted.

"But the horses!" Father reminded them as he rose to his feet.

"Tobe and Giddle are out there in the barn," they explained breathlessly.

"But Nellie and Cap are running around the yard still pulling the wagon. You're going to have a runaway yet!"

"Tobe and Giddle will get them," Dan insisted. "Don't go out there, Father. The wolves were right behind us."

When Mattie and Jake heard this, they quickly stepped inside the house. Mary and Lydia crowded in too and slammed the door shut. Father pulled on his boots and despite Dan's warning, ran out of the house and to the barn. Those inside the house could hear him shouting, "Wow! Whew! Get on!" to scare the wolves away, and they had to chuckle in spite of themselves.

"I tell you it isn't funny!" Dan insisted. "Those wolves were right behind us all the way from the mountains to here. We were so afraid we wouldn't make it before they attacked us." His breathing was still labored, and he found it hard to talk. "I don't know why we didn't take the gun along."

"Why did they follow you?" Jake asked.

Dan, Ezra, and Harry looked at each other. None of them spoke for some time. Finally Dan began the story.

"Well . . . we were piddling around this afternoon. We spent some time sightseeing and climbed a mountain. It started getting dark before we got back to the horses, so it was late when we started for home. We were still coming out of the mountains when we heard a wolf call."

Just then the door opened, and Tobe and Giddle entered with Father soon following. They sank into the kitchen chairs, white-faced and shaken, and asked for something to eat. Mother hurriedly set bowls around for them and put a large kettle of bean soup on the table.

"Come, boys," she motioned to Dan, Harry, and Ezra. "You can tell us the rest while you eat."

They wasted no time in sitting to the table. A bear had taken their meat the night before and left them with nothing to eat all day.

After they bowed their heads in silent prayer, Mary urged them to continue the story.

"Did you tell them you answered the wolf's call?" Dan asked Tobe.

Tobe chuckled, "I guess we'll know better next time."

"That's for sure!" Harry said.

"Why? What happened?" Mary wanted to know.

Tobe picked up the reporting. "When we answered their calls, they started to get closer and closer. Soon we realized they were following us, and the horses got scared. Before we knew it, they began running for all they were worth. We couldn't hold them back. And the faster the horses went, the faster the wolves came. They were so close we could see their teeth. I tell you—we were running for our lives!"

"Yeah, and the wagon was bouncing so bad we were afraid it might tear up," Dan added.

"If it would have broken up, we would have been sunk," Harry said. He took another serving of soup and asked for more water.

Mother refilled their glasses and began heating more milk. It was obvious they would soon have the bowl of bean soup emptied. She stirred some flour into a beaten egg to make rivels, small clumps that tasted like noodles when cooked. She added them to the hot milk.

"Where are the wolves now?" Mattie asked.

"I think they turned around and went back when the boys stopped here," Father said. "I didn't hear anything when I was outside. But by the way the horses were shaking, I know they weren't running from their imagination. I doubt that the wolves meant to attack them. They just thought it was a friendly race."

"Friendly race!" Tobe snorted. "They didn't sound very friendly to me."

"Well, I really don't think they intended to eat you up," Father reassured them.

"Maybe not us, but they would have attacked the horses."

"In any case, we'd sure rather be having supper at home than being supper for the wolves."

Father did not argue. He knew the boys had been badly frightened.

That evening as Mattie lay in bed and tried to sleep, she thought about the wolves alone on the prairie. They were probably jogging back to their dens or nests or wherever wolves sleep, and thinking about the wild-goose chase they had just had. *At least*, she thought, *life is not boring here in New Mexico. If it isn't pleasant, at least it's exciting.*

12

Working Out

MATTIE STOOPED to take eight loaves of bread from the oven. The sun was high in the sky and warming the whole kitchen like a bake oven. She wiped the sweat from her forehead with the back of her sleeve and put another eight loaves into the oven.

It would be a hot day, and she wanted to finish baking as soon as possible. It took twelve loaves of bread each week to feed the D. Y. Bontrager family.

Word had spread quickly that Crist Borntragers had girls old enough to work out, so Mattie soon had her old job back of being the maid. She missed her family terribly. But like Mother always said, "If someone needs help, then we must do what we can." It would have been selfish to stay home just because she wanted to.

Mattie put the last of the dishes in the cupboard and tidied the cabinet. Next she swept the floor and began peeling potatoes for dinner. They could soak in cold water until time to fry, and this gave Mattie a head start on dinner.

By the time the last batch of bread was finished baking, she was ready to skip out of the kitchen and work on some sewing. It would be cooler in the living room, and mending was a never-ending chore. Sometimes Mattie wondered if the Bontrager boys never watched out for barbed-wire fences.

When the bread had cooled and it was time to begin preparing dinner, Mattie carried the soft, fresh loaves to the cellar. It was a deep hole dug beneath the house, with the entrance on the outside. A heavy wooden door covered the opening, slanting from the ground to about three feet up the side of the house. Mattie had to set the pan of bread on the ground to lift it and lay it back out of the way.

She descended the steps to the cellar's dark coolness and smelled the wonderful aroma of hams and bacon. A fat, bearlike barrel sat in the corner, waiting for the fragrant loaves of bread. She lifted the lid and gently laid the loaves inside, being careful not to mash them. Then she returned the lid and went back up the stairs to the bright sunshine.

That night after everyone was asleep, someone—or something—crept into the cellar and stole two hams and several loaves of bread. No one heard a sound or suspected it until Mattie sent one of the little boys to the cellar to bring up a bacon for breakfast.

"Mattie!" he shouted as he rounded the side of the house and practically flew in the kitchen door. "Somebody stole a bunch of the bread you baked yesterday—and two hams!"

"What?!" she asked as she turned to him.

"Yeah. Somebody stole some of your bread and the hams."

Without a word, Mattie hurried down the steps and threw back the cellar door as though it were a feather. She rushed down the narrow steps and looked around. The lid of the barrel lay on the floor, but otherwise nothing was out of place.

"Is this how you found it?" she asked the little boy who had followed on her heels.

"Yep! The lid of the bread barrel was lying right there, and that's all you could see was wrong at first. Then when I picked up the bacon, I saw that two of the hams were gone."

"Was the cellar door open?"

"No," he said and shook his head.

Puzzled, Mattie lifted the lid and placed it on the barrel again. At the breakfast table, she told the Bontrager family of their discovery.

Immediately the older boys were full of ideas on how to catch the robber, and Mattie was sure if they had their way, she wouldn't have to worry about stolen bread again. Suzanne, their mother, told them to please be careful and not hurt anyone, to please not get hurt themselves, and please, please, don't speak so loudly.

That night the boys lay close by the windows, hoping the robber, or robbers, would return. But everything was quiet and all that was lost was a little sleep. The next night was quiet too, and soon the boys decided that whoever had stolen the hams and bread had only been passing through and would not return.

When Friday arrived, Mattie arose early to get the baking started before the sun rose too high. Once more she stirred up enough dough for twelve loaves of bread. With arms strong from milking many cows, she kneaded the dough until it was smooth and elastic. Then she shaped them perfectly into oblong rolls and placed them into buttered bread pans.

By the time they were baked and ready for the cellar, she had the house and kitchen in apple-pie order and was ready to prepare dinner. When she put the bread into the barrel, she remembered the thief the week before. She considered putting something heavy on the lid but decided against it. More than likely, it had been a cowboy in need of something to eat, and a ten-pound rock would not keep him out. She shrugged her shoulders and retraced her steps to the kitchen.

But that night the thief struck again. Nearly all the bread was taken this time, and just as before, it was done so quietly that no one heard it. Now the boys decided to sleep by the doorway. Surely they would hear someone walking past from there. But again, nothing happened, and the robber was still free.

The next week on bread-baking day, the boys decided to sleep by the door before the robber had a chance to get the bread. By now they were sure it was an animal that smelled Mattie's freshly baked bread.

To their advantage, the moon was almost full and rose early. They pulled their quilts and blankets close to the open doorway and lay still, as though asleep. Mattie slept on the living-room couch. Even though she had no privacy, she was too tired to care. She soon fell asleep.

Suddenly she was awakened by loud snickering and a scrambling of feet. She looked toward the kitchen door just in time to see the four older boys dive out the doorway.

Then there was a terrible howling of many dogs as they screamed and screeched and scratched to get away from the boys, who were severely meting out justice. Away they went, yapping and baying in terror, until they could only be only heard far in the distance.

Then Mattie heard a muffled thump . . . thump . . . thump. She guessed the boys were putting rocks on the cellar door. She turned over and fell back to sleep.

The next morning they excitedly told the family about the pack of dogs they had chased off. But with the heavy rocks on the cellar door, they were sure no dog could open it now.

To their surprise, when Mattie baked bread the next week, the rocks were removed and their bread was stolen again. This time the boys decided to try another trick. They rigged up a trap and hid it just inside the cellar door.

That night they lay by the open doorway as before, waiting for the dogs to come. All was quiet and Mattie was nearly asleep when suddenly there arose an ear-splitting howling and screeching. There was definitely a dog caught in the boys' trap.

The boys scrambled out the door, and Mattie got up to watch the action. Two of them were doubled over with laughter while two others wrestled with the dog to pin him down. She chuckled to herself and wondered what they were planning to do with him.

Soon one of the boys ran back to her and asked for some tin cans. She hurried to the kitchen and in the semidarkness found three. Without a word, he grabbed them from her and ran back to the cellar.

Mattie watched from the doorway as the boys hurriedly tied a long piece of twine to the dog's tail and spaced the three tin cans about five inches apart at the end. Then they carefully lifted the cellar door and opened the trap.

The dog jumped and howled when he suddenly realized he

was free. With a terrified scream, he bounded across the prairie in the same direction the other dogs had gone.

Howling and screeching, he nearly flew along the ground with the tin cans bumping and banging behind him. Occasionally they hit a clump of grass or a pile of dirt that sent them bouncing high and hit him on his back. This would wrench another volley of screams from him and a fresh burst of speed. Mattie couldn't help chuckling, and the boys were slapping their knees and rolling on the ground laughing.

From that night until Mattie was finished working for the Bontragers, not another loaf of bread was stolen and the boys were ever so proud of their remedy. Mattie had enjoyed working for them, but she eagerly looked forward to going home, too. As far as she knew, no one else was aware that she was coming, so maybe she would be able to stay home for several weeks this time.

One of the older boys took her home in their wagon. Just as they pulled into the yard, she noticed a cloud of dust on the horizon.

"Looks like someone is coming." The boy pointed toward the dust cloud.

"Yep." Mattie nodded as she lifted her suitcase from the wagon bed. "Probably Father or one of the boys."

She turned toward the house and saw Lydia standing in the doorway with a happy smile on her face. Turning to the boy, she waved and told him good-bye. Then she wearily walked to the house and set her suitcase just inside the door.

"So you're home!" Mother smiled at her from the kitchen where she was washing beans for supper.

"Sure am," Mattie sank onto the couch and asked Lydia where Mary was.

"She's working for Tobe's."

"Oh," Mattie nodded. "What have you been doing?"

Lydia looked at Mother, and they laughed together. "We haven't been doing anything, have we, Mother?"

Mother laughed and shook her head. "Not a thing."

Actually, they had been very busy getting the pinto beans ready for threshing, and Mother was glad to have Mattie at home to help. Father and the boys mowed the beans. After they were dry, Mother and Lydia had been putting them on piles for the threshing machine.

Just then a dusty Model T, with no top and its fenders rusted and peeling paint, chugged into the yard and stopped with a cough and a sputter.

"Oh, that must be what we saw out on the prairie a while ago," Mattie said, rising to her feet and looking out the window. A strange man climbed out of the car and walked up to the door. He took off his cap and smoothed his hair. Mother dried her hands on her apron and went to greet him while Mattie and Lydia listened quietly inside.

"Are you Mrs. Borntrager?" he asked.

"Yes, I am," Mother answered. Mattie thought she sounded funny, speaking English.

"Somebody told me you have girls that go around helping people who are in need."

Mother only nodded.

"My wife is very sick, and we need someone to do the washing. We have four children, and my wife's mother is there to do the cooking, but she's not strong enough to do the washing, and I'm busy trying to get the beans cut. So um . . . I was wondering if one of your girls could come and help us get the washing done. We haven't washed in about four weeks. . . ." His voice trailed off.

Mattie's heart sank. She had been planning to stay at home for a while, and now, she wasn't home five minutes before someone needed her.

"Yes. Our oldest girl is at home right now, and she can help you," Mattie heard Mother say.

Mother turned toward Mattie and asked if she could just take her suitcase as it was.

Mattie motioned for Mother to come to her. She wanted to talk to her but didn't want the man to hear.

"Do I have to go, Mother?"

"They really need help, Mattie."

"But we don't even know this man."

"I know. But if they haven't washed in over a month, they really need someone to help."

"But how do we know we can trust him?" Mattie fought back tears.

"We just have to, Mattie," Mother insisted.

So Mattie went with the stranger, sincerely hoping that Mother was right.

The Model T rolled across the ground so easily—even without a horse to pull it. There were no roads, so the man just struck off across the prairie at a westerly angle. Mattie wondered if he knew where he was going. But then she remembered that she had thought the same thing when Father brought them home from Springer, the night they had arrived from Kansas. Yet somehow they had arrived at home.

The sun was sinking low in the west and the air was already cooling. Suddenly they swerved sharply to the right.

"Snake," explained the man.

He stopped the car, got out, picked up a large rock, then drove back to find the snake. It was still coiled in the same spot. The man drew the Model T alongside it and stopped. He moved the gearshift into neutral, then picked up the big rock and stood on the seat.

Mattie peered over the side of the car door and was surprised to find the largest rattlesnake she had ever seen. It was nearly as big around as the top of her arm. The man lifted the rock high over his head and threw it down with all his strength. It smashed into the snake's head with a sickening crunch, and the snake writhed in anguish. After a few minutes, it lay still in death.

The man jumped over the car door and kicked it. When it didn't move, he picked up the rock and threw it onto the snake's head again. Then, satisfied that it was dead, he didn't bother to open the car door, but stepped nimbly over it, put the car into gear, and drove away. Mattie shuddered to think what a snake like that could have done to someone walking or to a horse. She was glad to be in an automobile.

After they had driven across the prairie for quite some time, she suddenly noticed the top of a windmill rising over a dip in the land. The man turned the steering wheel sharply, and the next instant they were hurtling down over a steep hillside. His farm lay at the bottom.

She wondered why he had put his farm buildings in such an unlikely place. Surely it must be hotter in the summertime with no breezes off the prairie to cool them. Maybe it had been winter when he found the place, and the steep hillside had seemed to be a natural protection from the wild blizzards that blew.

They rolled to a stop in front of a small house. Four young children, as dirty as any she had ever seen, stood in the doorway. They looked at Mattie cautiously, and suddenly Mattie was glad she had come. Certainly this family was in need of her help.

An elderly woman stood at the stove stirring a pot of beans. A piece of tin was propped against the stove to keep the door closed. The room was tidy, but dirty and in need of a good scrubbing. The little children minded their grandmother well and worked quickly, setting the table and helping her get supper on.

The man showed Mattie where she was to sleep and, again, it was on the couch. *Whose couch would she sleep on tomorrow night?* she wondered. She laid her black bonnet on the mantel and the suitcase on a chair close by. Then the grandmother called her to the table for supper.

The children began helping themselves to the food as soon as they sat down. So Mattie quietly bowed her head to pray, and when she finished, she discovered they had bowed their heads, too.

That evening Mattie ate the best biscuits she had ever tasted in her life. The food was not plentiful, but what little was there, was simply delicious. The children ate silently, and the father spoke only when spoken to, which was not often.

Only the grandmother visited with Mattie, so she asked her

what was wrong with her daughter.

"She has dropsy and keeps going from bad to worse," the grandmother answered gravely.

"Well, maybe just knowing the children have clean clothes and are bathed will help her feel better," said Mattie.

The grandmother nodded sadly and nothing more was said about the mother. Soon the father left the table, and Mattie knew it was a painful experience for him.

Early the next morning Mattie arose and began gathering the clothes and sorting them. The man brought a large washtub into the kitchen and set it on the stove. While it was heating, he carried water from the pump to the tub. Then he set another tub in the yard and carried rinse water to it.

Mattie stripped the beds and with the grandmother's help, changed the sick mother's bedsheets. When the water was hot, the man helped her carry the steaming tub to the yard.

Mattie found the washboard in the pantry and began the long task of scrubbing the clothes and wringing them out. She washed the sheets and spread them on top of a pile of deer antlers to dry. Then she washed the towels and underwear and nightclothes. Last of all, she washed the filthy pants, shirts, and dresses of the children, and the father's overalls.

By noon she had finished washing the clothes and was ready to bathe the children. The grandmother helped with the two little ones. Then she and Mattie took a washbasin, bathed the sick mother, and put fresh clothes on her. Finally, after everyone was bathed, she washed the dirty clothes they had been wearing.

After dinner, Mattie swept the kitchen and, with a stiff straw broom, began scrubbing the rough plank floor. She sloshed water on the floor and scrubbed and scrubbed. Then she swept the dirty water out the door and began the process all over again.

By evening the floor was dry, the clothes were dry, and everything was shining clean. The dirty water seemed thick enough to cut. With a good, satisfied feeling, Mattie dumped it out to water the young pear tree in the yard.

That evening, the biscuits the grandmother baked were extra

light and fluffy, and Mattie wished she could have such biscuits every day. The children seemed happier, the grandmother was talkative, the father smiled, and Mattie was so glad she had come.

13

Loco in New Mexico

TAKE A STEP, . . . PULL yourself up. Take another step,
. . . pull yourself up. It was hard work climbing Hogback, yet it
was the primary entertainment for the Amish youth.

Hogback was a steep and rocky mountain which was flat on
top and nearly a mile long and a mile high. The young people
loved climbing it and often took a picnic lunch along to enjoy
from the top. Today the boys had brought a crowbar to loosen
some of the rocks at the top and send them down the mountain-
side. It seemed to be a harmless sport and great fun.

Mattie carried a small basket of sandwiches, plates, and glasses. And Ida, the girl Jake had his eye on, carried another one
filled with pickled beets, cucumbers, and oranges. Jake carried a
jug of cold tea, and Mattie knew that his load was the heaviest.
When they reached the top at last, a strong wind was blowing
and made it difficult to lay out their dinner. But it did not damp-
en their spirits.

They could see way over the countryside, over the ripened
fields of oats and pinto beans hanging luxuriously full, over the
wide, wide prairie to the distant purple Rocky Mountains. And
then, they could see down, down, down to the prairie floor be-
low where a few cows grazed. It was beautiful.

Mattie peeled her orange and savored its tangy flavor. She listened to the young people talking and laughing around her and
sometimes joined in the fun. It amused her that Jake was show-
ing interest in Ida. He sat next to her and was accommodating to
her needs. To think it was Jake! Jake—who always said he'd nev-

er get married. Jake—in love with a girl. Mattie smiled.

After they finished eating, the girls began gathering up the scraps and putting their mess away while the boys disappeared behind some large rocks. Soon, Mattie heard them shouting and looked up just in time to see a large boulder roll down the side of the mountain. It picked up speed as it went, shearing off young trees and sending clouds of dust billowing upward. When it hit the prairie floor, it bounced once before rolling to a stop.

"Come quick," said Ida as she closed the lids tightly on the pickle jars and stuffed them into the basket. "Let's go watch the boys."

So the girls hurried to where the boys were prying rocks loose and letting them roll down the mountain. Then they loosened a huge one and, after much pushing and pulling, managed to get it to the edge.

Just as they pushed it over the edge and it began to roll, a cow walked innocently out from beneath a ledge at the foot of the mountain. Then another followed her, and soon several more. The girls screamed and everyone stood petrified with fear.

Half-grown trees, with trunks six to eight inches in diameter, were whacked off as the huge boulder hurtled over them. It hit other rocks and started an avalanche of smaller ones flying ever closer to the herd of cattle.

While the young people watched in terror, the cows suddenly ran away, apparently hearing the rocks coming. The next instant the largest rock crashed down on the very spot the cows had been walking only seconds earlier. A shower of smaller rocks pelted them and sent them bucking and galloping across the prairie.

A great sigh of relief swept through the crowd on top of the mountain. Their eyes met, and for once, they were not laughing.

"What if it had been a person?" Giddle spoke the thought they all were thinking.

"We'd better not do that again," Harry said. "That was too close for comfort."

It was a somber group that proceeded down the mountain

that afternoon and never again did they push rocks over the side.

The next day was Sunday and time to have church at Jacob T.'s home. There were six Amish families living in New Mexico now, and the church was growing. Father insisted that as long as the weather cooperated, and they continued to have good crops, more people would move in. Miles and miles of fences had been stretched and roads built.

Mr. Pittman, a neighbor to the west, had opened a store and sold most of the staples they needed. Now they seldom went to Gladstone or Mills to do business. Soon New Mexico would be just as civilized as Kansas. Maybe even more so.

Mr. Pittman asked Father if one of his girls could work for him during the busy season leading up to Christmas. So, again, Mattie was the one to go. He made lots of taffy, peppermint patties, and other Christmas candy, and his wife helped take care of customers. They lived in an upstairs apartment, and the store was downstairs.

The day Mattie stepped inside the front door, she immediately fell in love with the store. Mrs. Pittman smiled at her from where she stood behind the counter.

"Are you Mattie Borntrager?" she asked.

"Yes, I am." Mattie felt awkward speaking English.

"We sure are glad to see you. I've gotten so far behind with my work that I'm afraid you'll despair when you see the apartment."

"Oh, no." Mattie laughed.

"Just as soon as I get caught up here, I'll take you upstairs and show you around," Mrs. Pittman said.

Mattie watched Mr. Pittman as he kneaded a batch of taffy. He worked on a large marble slab, pushing down hard on the ball of candy, then turning it over and pushing again. When he was satisfied that it was of the right consistency, he picked it up and threw it over a stainless steel hook on the wall.

He pulled it down to the table, then threw it up over the hook again. Over and over he pulled it down and threw it back up. Soon it became smooth and white.

When it was nearly finished, he picked up a small bottle with a cork pushed into its top. Uncorking it, he poured a small amount of clear liquid onto the taffy. Then he reached back to a wooden shelf and picked up another bottle of yellow food coloring. He opened the top and gently shook out three drops. Mattie guessed the first bottle was flavoring, probably lemon or banana, since he was coloring it yellow. She wished she could taste some.

The store was filled with barrels of crackers, rice, flour, salt, sugar, and pinto beans. There were tins of leavening, cinnamon, and cocoa. But only three bolts of fabric were on the shelf, and Mattie didn't care for any of them. Saddles, bridles, and other tack hung along the west wall.

An Indian woman was at the counter, wanting to bargain a brightly colored hair ribbon for sugar. Mrs. Pittman patiently explained to her that she must pay for it with money. Mattie began growing impatient and wondered if she could find something to do if she went upstairs. She decided against it and walked outside to look around.

There was a long wooden bench just outside the door, but no one sat on it. She supposed people would come and lounge there later in the day. The air smelled dry and dusty, as though a cattle train had just passed through.

The Indian woman noiselessly opened the door and slipped out. Mattie watched as she walked across the prairie, not moving any part of her body except her legs and feet. Those were hidden beneath her long, flowing skirt, so she appeared to glide across the ground.

At long last Mrs. Pittman led Mattie up a dark, narrow flight of stairs to their apartment. They could hear children's voices as they ascended. When they stepped into the room, the children grew quiet and shy, and Mattie felt conspicuous in her large black bonnet and shawl. She immediately removed them and laid them on a chair.

Dirty dishes lay piled in the sink, but otherwise the house was orderly. The three children, from three to seven years old, looked clean and well cared for. While Mrs. Pittman was telling her what needed to be done, Mattie decided she would be working for an efficient woman, but one that would not be hard to please.

"First, you can clean the oven. Then tomorrow we'll try to get an earlier start and do the laundry." Mrs. Pittman rolled her eyes playfully and threw up her hands. She told Mattie not to be shocked at the mountain of dirty clothes and said she believed they had dirtied every stitch they owned.

Mattie laughed and relaxed. She would feel right at home here, that was sure.

The early snows of winter fell before Thanksgiving, and business slacked off for a few days. But when the sun returned, people came in record numbers. Soon even Mattie helped in the store almost every day. The children played contentedly in the back of the store, sometimes helping their father wrap the little pieces of candy in shiny cellophane wrappers and laying them attractively in the glass showcase.

It was an exciting time for the family, and Mattie enjoyed working for them. Mr. Pittman had a reputation for excellent candy. People came from miles around, as far away as Mills, twenty-eight miles to the south, to purchase his sweets.

One day Mr. Pittman announced that he was running low in chocolate and Mrs. Pittman would need to go to Gladstone to get more. So the next day she and the children went to town, twelve miles away. Mattie agreed to keep the store. She had worked in it enough that she felt comfortable with the customers.

The morning passed uneventfully, and Mattie swept the floors and straightened the items on the shelves. A cowboy walked in and Mattie helped him with his purchases: a bag of coffee, a small bag of sugar cubes, and some rice. Soon after he left a young Indian boy entered the store and asked for a "stumpus."

"What did you say?" Mattie asked. She listened closely when he repeated it.

"A stumpus."

Mattie looked all around the store, trying to decide what a stumpus was.

"Say it real slow," she suggested.

"Stumpus," he repeated, not blinking an eye.

"Stumpus?"

He nodded his head. Again she looked all around the store, wondering what he could possibly mean. She didn't want to interrupt Mr. Pittman, but eventually asked him to come and see if he knew what the little boy wanted.

"Can I help you with anything?" Mr. Pittman asked, bending close to hear.

"I want stumpus," the boy answered seriously.

"A . . . stumpus?"

Again the boy nodded.

Mr. Pittman looked at Mattie and shook his head. Then he had an idea.

"Is there one in this store?" he asked the little Indian.

The boy nodded his head.

"Can you show us?"

The boy looked all around the store, then walked over to Mr. Pittman's desk. There he stood and solemnly stared at the mountain of papers. Suddenly, he reached up and took a letter from one of the pigeonholes and pointed to the stamp.

"Oh—a stamp!" Mattie exclaimed. She and Mr. Pittman exchanged amused glances. Then Mattie led the boy to the counter and handed him a stamp. He gave her two pennies, warm from clutching them tightly in his hand. Then he turned stiffly and moved silently to the door. Not until he was out of hearing distance did she and Mr. Pittman share a good laugh over it.

That afternoon, while business was slow, Mattie pulled a chair up to the window and stared at the barren landscape. A lone horse was walking with an odd gait toward the store. When he came closer, she saw he was very thin and looked half-starved.

The horse walked thirstily toward the water tank. When he was about five feet from it, he stopped and pretended to drink. Mattie wondered why he didn't move up just a little farther and get a real drink, then suddenly realized that he was loco, crazy. He had eaten too many locoweeds and was turned out to forage for himself on the prairie.

Mattie felt sorry for him and wished he would get closer to the tank and drink. After standing there for a long time and pretending to drink, he turned and, in his peculiar gait, walked back out to the prairie from where he had come.

Life in New Mexico was harsh and taught its lesson well— well enough that Mattie could not forget the loco horse. She knew he would probably die from his own foolishness.

14

Mirages

FATHER HAD TWO WAGONLOADS of fat hogs to take to Mills, a town twenty-eight miles to the south. So Giddle, Jake, Mattie, and Mary went along, not only to help drive the wagons, but to do some shopping as well. Mother had given the girls enough money to get dress material while they were there.

It had been two years since they had been to town, and longer than that since they had gotten new dresses. Father, Mattie, and Mary traveled in the lead wagon while Jake and Giddle drove the back one. It would be an exciting day.

They started on their journey long before sunup, while the air was cool and fresh and the stars hung brilliant and low. But before long, daylight pushed the stars back into the morning sky. It was sure to be a hot day. However, they had brought plenty of water for themselves and knew of a place along the way where they could water the horses and hogs. They were not planning to come back that day but would sleep at a bunkhouse that was open for anyone who needed it.

The sun came up, fiery hot, scorching the prairie and everything upon it, including the two lone wagons filled with fat hogs. Mattie and Mary pulled their black bonnets forward as far as they could. Father and the boys pulled their straw hats low over their faces to shield themselves from the hot sun. They drank sparingly of the water they had brought along.

The horses walked slower and slower, yet Father didn't push too hard in the heat. Rivers of sweat ran down their backs, and their tails swished flies. Mattie knew they were more miserable than she, and she felt sorry for them. The hogs grunted and squirmed and tried to stand up, only to fall back upon their knees. Then, with a flop and a sigh, they laid still, panting like dogs.

By noon Father began earnestly searching for the place where they could stop for water. The horses were heaving into the harness as though it were their dying effort. But still they plodded on. Suddenly Mary stood up on the floorboard and announced that there were buildings ahead. Mattie looked in the direction she pointed, but saw only empty prairie, with heat waves glimmering on the horizon.

"Where do you see buildings?" she asked, her tongue thick from the heat.

"Over there." Mary pointed to the east.

"You're seeing things," Father said, and Mattie thought it sounded as though he were suffering from the heat as well.

"Oh! . . ." Mary's voice trailed off and she slowly sat down. "I thought sure there were buildings over there." She continued looking in the direction she had seen them. "I know I saw some."

"Sometimes it looks that way, but it's just a mirage and isn't really true," Father said.

He realized they were thirsty and needed cool water and rest. "Drink more of the water now and maybe we'll find some for the animals before too long."

By now the horses were walking as though they could not go much farther. They moved slower and slower until Mattie began to wonder if they would soon stop. Suddenly, Father stood in the wagon and looked hard to the southeast.

"There it is . . . over there," he announced.

But try as they might, the rest of them could not see anything that resembled water.

"Yes! I'm sure it's a windmill," he insisted.

Mattie and Mary stood up, too, but could see only miles and miles of wide empty prairie.

"Now *you're* seeing things, Father," they said. He looked long and hard before deciding they were right. He was seeing a mirage, too. Would they ever find water?

Then, just when they were almost in despair, they sighted buildings. This time they were sure they were not seeing a mirage. Even the horses quickened their pace as they smelled water. Soon they were nearly running, and it did not take long to get there. The buildings were abandoned, but signs were everywhere that many people used this windmill for water.

The horses drank deep and long, and the hogs pushed and jostled each other to get to the water bucket that Jake and Giddle set in the wagons for them. Mary slung her bonnet over a fence post, pushed up her sleeves, and plunged her arms into the water, right next to Nellie's head. Nellie only blinked at her and Mary laughed.

"Wheee!" she giggled. Then she splashed water over her sunburned face and rubbed her parched lips. "Come, Mattie," she beckoned. Mattie wasted no time in getting her bonnet untied and hung on a fencepost too. Then she joined Mary at the water tank, soaking her arms and washing her face.

Father and the boys threw their hats on the ground and began cooling off alongside the horses and Mattie and Mary. No one spoke, for their lips were dry and swollen, their tongues thick. They drank directly from the waterspout—all they wanted. Then Father filled the water jug, and they sat in the shade of the wagon to eat the sandwiches Mother had prepared. When at last they were ready to go again, the horses seemed rested and the hogs were quiet.

But as soon as wagons began to roll, the sun again seemed to burn directly through their skin. After several hours Mattie wiped her lips and discovered they were bleeding. She tried not to lick them, but with the sun and wind drying them so, it was hard not to. She looked at Mary and saw her lips were cracked and bleeding too. They were swollen and made her face look unnatural.

Turning to look at Father, Mattie saw him glance at her out of the corners of his eyes, and she thought he was laughing at her.

But his eyes were mere slits and she couldn't be sure. Suddenly their pitiful situation struck her as being funny and she tried not to giggle.

Mary looked sharply at her, then giggled too. Father looked sideways at them through his slitted eyes, and this struck them as being hilarious. Soon they were shaking with laughter and covering their mouths with their hands, trying to keep them from cracking more. Even though they couldn't talk, at least they could laugh—or try to.

Suddenly, Giddle yelled from the wagon behind them, "Get her!"

Mattie, Mary, and Father turned quickly to see Jake dive off their wagon and race after a sow that had gotten out and was running away.

"Go help him, Mattie!" Father shouted.

Instantly, Mattie was out of the wagon and running after the wayward pig, too. It ran swiftly on its short legs, turning first one direction and then another. Soon Mary joined them and they ran this way and that, trying to head the pig back toward the wagons—only to have her break between them at the last minute and head out to the prairie again.

Jake noticed a buffalo hollow and told the girls to chase the sow into it. He picked up a weathered piece of wood and threw it at her, hitting her on the leg. She squealed and picked up speed, running toward the hollow. The girls ran as fast as they could, waving their arms and screaming wildly. Down into the hollow she went, with Jake close behind.

Just as the sow slowed to go up the other side, he lunged and grabbed her back leg. Kicking and squealing, she nearly loosened his hold on her. But in another second, he grabbed her with his other hand and wrestled her to the ground. Mary quickly sat on her head to keep her from getting up.

Panting and heaving, Jake told Mattie to go back to the wagons and tell Father and Giddle to come. But even before she appeared at the top of the hollow, Father and Giddle were there. In only a second, they jumped down and Father told Mattie to hold the horses. Then all together Father and the boys pushed and pulled the errant sow to her feet and up the steep sides of the hollow to the waiting wagons.

They lifted the tailgate, placed one end on the ground, and tried to make the pig walk up it into the wagon. But instead, she tried to break away, and they soon saw they might lose more pigs if they didn't get the tailgate closed. Father hurriedly put it back in place and instructed Mattie to take the other wagon and drive it down into the buffalo hollow. She was to back it up until the wagon bed was level with the ground where they were standing.

Jake and Giddle pushed the sow down and sat on top of her until Mattie got the wagon into the right position. Father removed the tailgate again and kept the other pigs from crowding too close and making a break for freedom.

Jake and Giddle carefully guided the pig to the wagon. But just as she stepped onto it, Cap shifted his position, jerked the wagon, and all the pigs fell, squealing in panic. Somehow, Jake and Giddle kept the large sow under control, and Father didn't let any of the others get out—but not without shouting to Mattie to "HOLD THE WAGON STILL!!"

Mattie felt ashamed for not having watched Cap more closely. She carefully backed him up until the wagon bed was level with the ground again. Then she held firmly to his bridle until Jake and Giddle had the pig pushed onto the wagon and the tailgate was securely closed. How she had gotten out in the first place, they didn't know. But one thing was sure: they would watch them more closely.

As they turned back toward town, they wondered if they would get to the stores before they closed. The sun was quite low, and the horses were not moving very fast. But before long, Mills was on the horizon, and they relaxed, knowing they were in plenty of time.

Father left Mattie and Mary at the General Store while he, Giddle, and Jake went on to the railroad to sell the hogs. As the girls stepped up onto the porch, they suddenly felt horribly dirty and out of place. But they were there now and there was nowhere else to go, so they stepped uncertainly inside the door. Two women were behind the counter, chattering like chipmunks. But when they saw Mattie and Mary standing there, not knowing what else to do, they hurried over to them.

"Can we help you, girls?" one of them asked. Then she saw their sunburned faces and swollen lips.

"Oh, you poor girls! Where have you been?" she wailed. Turning to the other lady, she told her, "Quick, get the salve!"

Mattie and Mary felt embarrassed as the two women fussed over them like mother hens and rubbed their sunburned faces and lips with cool salve. It was soothing to their sore mouths, and soon they were able to smile and speak plainly. But not until the two women were satisfied that Mattie and Mary felt better, did they offer to get the items they wanted to purchase.

"We'd like some dress material," Mattie informed them.

"Any particular kind?" the one lady asked.

"Something dark and solid colored," Mattie said.

The two ladies bustled about. They took several bolts of fabric from the high shelves and placed them on the counter. Mattie and Mary felt the fabrics and looked over each bolt but couldn't decide which they wanted. Finally Mary chose a deep wine-colored piece and told the lady to cut five yards from the bolt. Mattie wanted both the deep forest green and a navy blue.

"But you already have a blue one. Why don't you get the green?" Mary suggested.

"I guess you're right," Mattie said. "But I like that blue so well."

"Then get it if that's what you want," Mary prodded her.

Mattie wished things were as simple as Mary made it sound. Mary always knew exactly what she wanted while Mattie couldn't make up her mind. The lady finished cutting and folding Mary's fabric and stood patiently waiting for Mattie to decide.

"Ach! I guess I'll just take the blue." She suddenly pushed the bolt of fabric toward the lady.

"Well, if you want the green too, why don't you take both?" the lady asked.

"Oh, no," Mattie shook her head. "Mother only gave us enough money for one. And I think I'll be happier with the blue."

So the lady cut five yards of the blue fabric and carefully folded it into a small neat square. Then she took both pieces to the cash register and wrapped them in brown paper. Finally she tied them together with a length of narrow white string.

"That will be ten yards of fabric for thirty cents a yard . . . which makes a total of $3.00," she said as she punched the small round keys on the cash register and turned a ivory handle on the side. A long drawer slid open, and when Mattie handed the three dollar bills to the lady, she laid them gently in their proper compartment. Then she closed the drawer and thanked them for their business.

Mattie picked up the package and Mary followed her to the door. The other lady hurried to hold the door for them and warned them to keep their bonnets pulled forward on the way home, so the sun wouldn't hit them so directly. They smiled and thanked them. Father and the boys were nowhere in sight, so they waited on the porch until they arrived.

It was a relief to have all the pigs off the back of the wagons, and the ride toward home was a quiet one. The sun had long set by the time they arrived at the bunkhouse where they would spend the night. Mattie and Mary wished for a cool bath and clean sheets, but they wouldn't complain. At least they had bunks to sleep in and wouldn't have to spend the night on the hard-packed ground with the wolves.

The next morning they left before sunup and reached home soon after dinner. Never had Mattie been so glad to see their small adobe house, with plenty of food, plenty of water, and relief from the hot, hot sun.

Mattie's vacation did not last long. The next day D. Y. Bontrager rode up to the house and asked for Mattie's help again. "Millie Jones is there already, but we feel we need another girl, too," he said.

Millie, Mattie thought, *Oh, that will be fun!*

Mother turned to look at Mattie. Her face was beet-red and still a bit swollen. "Do you feel you could go?" she asked.

"Oh, sure," Mattie replied. "I feel all right." So Mattie packed her worn suitcase and went with D. Y.

Millie was working in the kitchen when Mattie arrived and smiled with pleasure when she walked in. They always enjoyed each other's company, and Mattie was glad to have someone else to work with.

"How long have you been here?" Mattie asked, after putting her suitcase and bonnet in the living room.

"Since Sunday."

"Have you been pretty busy?"

Millie's eyebrows shot up and she gave Mattie a sly wink. Mattie chuckled. She knew they would have plenty of work to keep both of them hopping. She rolled up her sleeves and asked for a dishpan and a paring knife. Millie reached up and took a pan from a high shelf. Then she told Mattie to look in a box underneath the cabinet for a knife.

"I'll peel these potatoes for you," she offered and began helping prepare the supper. The two girls visited as good friends, and how the time flew. It was so nice to have someone to work with, talk with, and laugh with.

Suzanne, the mother, had all she could handle in caring for her family of seven boys and two girls. Mattie and Millie seldom heard her scold the little ones, and it seemed as though the home ran smoothly. The children were quiet and obedient and Suzanne humble and sensitive.

Mattie and Millie stayed most of the summer, and every day was filled with work from sunup to sundown. Two hired boys also worked for the Bontragers, so there was much cooking, baking, and laundry to be done along with the gardening. But with someone like Millie to work with, every chore was easy and fun.

One evening while the two girls were washing the supper dishes, Millie noticed the water bucket was empty. Just to be silly, she pushed the bucket back against the wall and quipped,

"Said Peter to Paul, the water is all."

And to make it rhyme Mattie countered, "Said Paul to Peter, it isn't either."

The two burst out laughing, but then they noticed the family watching them curiously. Mattie and Millie knew they wouldn't understand the joke, and they tried to hush. But the harder they tried not to laugh, the funnier it became.

When the dishes were finally finished and the kitchen clean, they skipped out the back door and ran to the outhouse. It seemed a quarter of a mile away when they were in such a hurry, but after they reached it, they felt free to laugh until they could laugh no more.

Then they strolled over to some rocks, sat down, watched the stars come out, and talked until they were sure the family was asleep. The two hired boys slept in the living room along one wall, while Mattie and Millie slept along the other wall. So every evening the girls made sure the two boys were sleeping before they went to bed. It was their only way to be modest in such tight quarters.

Tonight the girls knew it was a little late when they returned to the house, but they were shocked to discover it was already past midnight. They tiptoed into the living room and slid beneath the sheets, hoping no one knew how long they had sat outside talking.

Mattie and Millie planned to work for the Bontragers until harvest, but plans changed, and all because of a toothache. One night Mattie felt a dull pain in her teeth. She didn't know if it was one tooth hurting or two. But they hurt badly enough that she could not fall asleep for a long time.

The next morning she told Suzanne about it, and Suzanne told her to go home if she wanted to. Mattie rubbed her cheek, not sure what to do. But the pain continued to worsen, and by late afternoon she decided to go home.

It was thirty miles to the nearest dentist, and she knew that she would not be able to go that far to pull her teeth. Father had a tooth pliers and pulled teeth for other people. He would pull hers if she asked him to. So D. Y. hitched up the buggy, and Mattie said good-bye to Millie and Suzanne and went home.

The autumn air was clear and cool, a blessed relief from the hot, dry summer they had endured. But Mattie didn't notice. Her head hurt from the top of her ear to her throat. Nothing seemed as important at that moment as getting the two aching teeth out of her mouth. But when she told Father of her predicament, he only looked the other way. He didn't like to pull teeth.

"Maybe it will feel better by morning. Why don't we wait and see?" he suggested.

"Oh, no, Father," Mattie begged. "These teeth have been hurting all day."

"But they often hurt worse in the evening and maybe if you get a good night's sleep, in your own bed, you'll feel better in the morning."

"Well . . . maybe so," she finally agreed.

But there was no sleep for Mattie that night. The entire side of her head raged with pain unmercifully. Never had a night seemed as long. But the next morning Father was still reluctant to pull her teeth. He went out to the field to work, leaving Mattie to suffer throughout the entire day.

But when he returned in the evening and saw her swollen cheek and bloodshot eyes, he knew that the time had come for him to do the task he so dreaded.

"Go outside," he told her. Then he went into the bedroom, opened the top bureau drawer, and got out the tooth pliers. Already, sweat beads were glistening on his forehead.

His hand trembled when he stepped up to her and touched her chin. She opened her mouth and squeezed her eyes shut tight. Unbidden tears trickled out. She felt him tighten his grip on the one tooth and gently tug at it. Because it had hurt so badly before, she felt no extra pain when he pulled on it now. She only wished he would hurry.

He loosened the tooth as gently as possible and then began to pull in earnest. Suddenly the pliers slipped off and hit the top of her mouth. But that didn't matter to Mattie. Nothing could be as bad as having those teeth in her mouth. Father tightened his grip again and pulled, this time succeeding in yanking the tooth out.

Then he loosened the other one and quickly had both teeth lying on the ground. Mattie looked up and saw the sweat pouring off his face. His clothes looked as though he just jumped out of the water tank. He was dripping wet. But she was smiling.

In no time at all, she changed her clothes, went to bed, and slept peacefully. Pulling those teeth had been harder on Father than on Mattie.

15

The Baby

MATTIE STRUGGLED against the bitter wind to reach the house. She wearily stepped inside the front door. All was quiet. The kitchen was warm and clean, but Mother was nowhere in sight. She looked out the window and saw Lydia bringing the cows up from the pasture. Her face was nearly buried in a thick woolen scarf.

Mattie debated about helping with chores, but then decided against it and began peeling potatoes for supper. She had been working for Jonas Mullets and was tired to the bone. Presently, Lydia pushed through the kitchen door and was surprised to find Mattie at home.

"So you're home!" Lydia said cheerfully. Her lips were almost too cold to talk.

"Yes," Mattie answered. "John just brought me. But where's Mother?"

"She's over at Tobe's. Mary went along."

"Nettie's having the baby?" Mattie's eyebrows shot up.

"Yep. Tobe came after Mother this morning already, but we haven't heard anything yet."

"Probably won't until this evening."

"Probably not."

Mattie turned back to the dry sink to finish peeling the potatoes, but Lydia stopped her. "Why don't you come and help us with the milking?"

"Mmm. . . . I'd better stay inside where it's warm," Mattie answered ruefully.

"Humphh!" Lydia snorted. "Those dishwater hands of yours could use some toughening up. Come on. I have to do the chores all by myself tonight, and it would go so much faster if you helped."

"Well, let me finish these potatoes, and then I'll come out," Mattie replied. It had been a long time since she helped with the chores at home, and it would be fun to milk with Lydia again. Not that she didn't do her share of milking. At most of the places where she worked, she helped with both the barn chores and the housework.

While Mattie and Lydia were milking, they exchanged bits of news and other items of interest. But neither of them mentioned what was heavy on their minds—Nettie and her baby. They hoped everything would go all right and the baby would be healthy. Many, many babies and their mothers died on the prairie, with no doctors to assist them and only mothers and neighbor women for midwives.

Not only did many women die here in New Mexico, but in other places as well. Several months earlier Nettie had received a letter from her family informing her of her mother, Katie's death. It had been a terrible shock, and all the letter stated was that she had died of dropsy. Because Nettie didn't say much about it, there were many unanswered questions in Mattie's mind.

Mother often helped with birthings and other illnesses, and usually Mattie didn't pay much attention to them. But because Nettie was Tobe's wife and a member of the family, and in the shadow of Katie's death, the danger seemed greater.

It was well past sundown when they heard a wagon approach and knew that Tobe and Mother were returning. Father anxiously opened the door to help Mother in, his eyes searching her face for clues to the events of the day. She was smiling as she ascended the steps in the chilly wind.

"What'd she have?" Lydia blurted out.

"A girl," Mother replied, setting her satchel of birthing supplies on the table.

"Everything went okay?" Father asked.

"Oh, yes. Nettie and the baby are both doing real good. I left Mary there to help out though. John and Crist can get into anything."

"I'll bet Nettie's tickled pink to have a girl after two lively boys," Mattie said.

"Guess what they named her," Mother said, smiling from ear to ear.

"Mary!" Lydia guessed. That was Mother's name as well as sister Mary's.

"Nope."

"Probably Katie—after Nettie's mom," Mattie said.

"Nope."

"Then tell us," Lydia prodded.

"It's *Mattie*."

Mattie was speechless. What a surprise! "Mattie?" she asked.

"Yes, Mattie." Mother smiled.

Mattie could hardly believe it. Now she couldn't wait to see the baby. Maybe tomorrow she would make a little dress with the scraps she had left from her new blue one. And maybe on Sunday they could take it over and see her little namesake. That night Mattie went to bed feeling light and happy and thinking how special it was to have a brand-new niece named after her.

Sunday dawned clear but cold. It was January and the prairie was locked in winter's icy grip. Icicles hung from the edges of the roof, some as thick as Mattie's wrist. Thin ones, dainty and fragile, necklaced the prairie, twinkling on miles and miles of barbed-wire fences.

No church services would be held because of the cold. So Mattie, Giddle, and Lydia asked Father if they could hitch Nellie to the buggy and visit Tobe's. Without a moment's hesitation, he consented, and they were off to get their wraps.

Father wasn't as concerned about cold weather as some people were. He always said it's the people who bundle up tightly and smother themselves in coats and scarves who get sick. Sometimes Mattie almost believed him.

She remembered how he had let Giddle go to school when he was only about four years old and it was snowing and blowing terribly. Mother wouldn't have let him go if Father hadn't said that he could. And Giddle did not get sick from it either. In fact, he never missed a day that entire school year, so the teacher had even given him a pearl-handled pocketknife on the last day of school.

Still, Mattie and Lydia put on several layers of garments and thick warm coats. Then they wrapped woolen scarves around their necks and faces. The wind could cut you to the bone if you weren't careful. Some people told of their noses freezing because they didn't keep them covered. It was so cold today that it seemed twice as far as the three miles it actually was.

They tied Nellie in the barn, covered her with a blanket, then hurried to the house. With a rapid knock, they burst through the doorway.

"Anybody home?" they called.

Tobe, who had been sleeping beside the stove, jumped in surprise. "Oh, it's you," he mumbled.

"Sleepyhead," Lydia teased.

"Hey, come in!" Mary arose from the table where she had been reading to John and Crist.

"We have baby." John slid off the chair where he had been sitting and hurried over to Mattie, hugging her legs and making it impossible for her to get her coat off. "We have baby," he repeated.

"You do?" Mattie knelt and put her arm around his thin shoulders. He nodded his head and smiled.

"Yep. We sure do," Crist agreed. "And she has your name," he pointed toward Mattie.

"Isn't that nice?" She smiled.

Mary went to the bedroom and soon returned with the baby. Mattie took the soft cotton-wrapped bundle in her arms and held her reverently. She didn't resemble the older children but looked a little more like Nettie.

Lydia told Mattie to hurry, finish holding the baby, so she

could have her turn. Tobe moved his chair closer to Giddle and wanted to hear the news from home. Crist and John tried to go into the bedroom to talk to their mother, but Mary gently took them aside and quieted them. The afternoon passed swiftly and pleasantly.

When it was time for the young people to leave, Mary saw another buggy across the prairie. Soon they recognized Blaze, Jake's horse. Likely he had Ida along. They were almost inseparable anymore, and the family expected them to announce their wedding soon.

When Jake knocked on the door, Mary let them in.

"You don't have to knock around here," Tobe said when they had entered and were taking off their coats. Mattie thought Jake acted embarrassed but couldn't be sure. He certainly didn't act around Ida the way he did at home. Maybe they weren't as close to getting married as the family thought. Ida seemed strangely quiet, and Jake laughed nervously about anything that was said.

They both held the baby and then gave her to Mary to take back to the bedroom. Nettie wasn't strong enough to be up yet, and Mattie felt they should go home. But just as they were preparing to leave, Jake cleared his throat and told them to stay. He had something he wanted to tell them, and he thought they would want to know.

Mattie sat down again and looked curiously at Lydia. Giddle winked and Mattie almost giggled. Tobe smiled and looked out the window. But Jake did not seem to notice and rubbed his hand over and over his leg while Ida twisted her handkerchief into a tight wad.

"Um . . . we just wanted you . . . uh, the family, to know that Ida here," and he jerked his thumb toward her, "and I are planning to get married."

All were silent. Jake continued to rub his leg, and Ida untwisted her handkerchief, only to twist it tight again.

Suddenly Tobe burst out laughing. "Well, it's about time!" he said in a loud voice so like Father's. It was exactly how he would have reacted.

"When are you getting married?" Mary asked.

Jake looked up and Ida smiled. "In March, I guess," Jake replied.

"Oh" was all Mary said.

"Well! That was worth staying for," Mattie announced, straightening her back. "The way Jake and Ida were acting, I thought they were going to tell us they were breaking up."

Ida laughed self-consciously, and Mattie wished she could feel more at ease with them. But in time, she was sure, Ida would be just like one of them.

"I suppose you'll be *Newehocke* (sitting alongside, bridesmaid)," Lydia said to Mattie on their ride home.

"Nay. It'll be Ola and Giddle, and Mary and Harry, probably."

"Nope! I bet it will be you and Ezra."

"Ach! Such an imagination!" Mattie snorted.

"Let's just wait and see," Lydia said.

Time passed quickly, with winter blowing into spring. Everyone was busy getting ready for the wedding. Mother pieced a comforter, and she and the girls quilted it in long stitches with crochet thread.

Then Mother sorted through her dishes and chose several bowls, a cake plate, and a glass pitcher to give to them. They were family keepsakes. Some of them were passed to her from her mother and her grandmother and some were from Father's mother. It was only fitting that the children should have some of them when they married.

And then there was sewing to do. As it turned out, Lydia had been right about Mattie being one of the *Newehocke*. She would be with Ezra, Ida's brother, and Mary would be with Harry, Ida's younger brother. So there were new dresses to make, and Mother was making Jake's suit.

Not much time was left to get ready, and all the work must be done secretly. No one in the community was to know about it until two weeks before the wedding. Then Abe Nissley, the minister, published them by simply announcing that Jake and Ida would be getting married in two weeks.

Now the work began in earnest. Because of the small community, it would not be a large wedding, as Tobe and Nettie's had been. But in spite of that, there was still lots of work to be done.

The day of the wedding was chilly, with a high, silvery sun. Mattie and Mary rode in Jake's buggy to Ida's home and took their places at the front of the room beside Ida. Mary sat to her left, and Harry and Ezra sat on the opposite side next to Jake. After the ceremony, tables were set up in the tiny living room for the reception.

Jake and Ida set up housekeeping just across the field from Mattie's home in a rented house. Many were the times they walked to each other's homes for the evening or to borrow a cup of sugar.

The summer before, 1922, had been rather dry, and the crops had not produced as usual. But this summer, 1923, was extremely dry. The prairie practically barren. Father was gloomy much of the time, and Mattie wondered what would happen if it didn't begin to rain. She heard that other men were thinking of moving back to Kansas. Inwardly she hoped Father would decide to move back, too, but at the same time she did not want him to lose everything he had worked so hard for.

She continued her stints as a maid for other people and wondered if that was to be her lot in life. It seemed to be an endless job, what with the many little faces to wash—faces of other mothers' children, and meals to cook—delicious meals for other mothers' families.

Would she never have her own little faces to wash and her own family to feed? Would she never have the privilege to rest with her babies in the afternoon as other mothers did? Would she never feel loved and cherished by her husband as these women were cherished?

But she was only twenty. There were many years left to settle down, she supposed. And yet . . . sometimes she wondered.

16

Sam

NINETEEN TWENTY-FOUR. Another year. Another drought. Another hot day. Heat weaves shimmered on the horizons, creating visions of pools of water where there was no water. Nothing grew. Cattle bellowed. Father worried. And Mattie wished they were anywhere but in New Mexico. What had happened that the rains no longer came? The bountiful crops they had grown the first years seemed like a farfetched dream now.

It was Sunday morning, and church services were to be held at the Noah Bontrager home. Mattie brushed her long brown hair. She parted it in the center, combed it straight back, and tied a long ribbon around her head. Next she crossed the ribbon under her chin and held the ends in her mouth while she flipped her hair up, pinned it at the top, and curled the ends beneath.

Taking the ends of ribbon from her mouth, she tied them at the nape of her neck. Then she settled her large black covering over her head and pinned it in place with two straight pins. The married women wore white and the unmarried girls wore black. She donned her blue Sunday dress, the one she wore every Sunday, and pinned her cape in place. It was a piece of cloth that she folded to create a triangle, pinning a corner on each side of the neck and a corner at the waist.

"Hurry up, Mattie!" Giddle called from the doorway.

Mary was combing twelve-year-old Lydia at the kitchen table, and Mattie knew that she was not ready either. Why Giddle picked on her, she didn't know. She pulled on her stockings and hurriedly stepped into her black shoes. They hurt her feet when she walked, and she was glad she didn't have to wear them every day. They were hot, too. She went to the kitchen and offered to finish combing Lydia.

It was quite a hassle getting everyone ready for church. Mother often said that she was more on time when the children were small than she was now.

The air was so humid this morning. The sun was shining so brightly and fierce that Mattie felt as though she must surely smell like a workhorse. The sky, that usually seemed to rise eternally higher and higher, now pressed down on them, threatening to smother every unfortunate creature on the prairie.

No one knew what the future held. But, unless rain fell and they could raise pinto beans and oats as they had before, they most certainly would need to move East again. Father had his farm completely paid for and was in better financial condition than some of the other families. But nevertheless, he stood in danger of losing everything he had brought with him from Kansas and had acquired in New Mexico.

Already Jake and Ida had moved back to Kansas, and Dan and Polly were talking of moving to Indiana. Mattie would have her twenty-first birthday in October, and she was considering going back to Kansas, too. She would be on her own then, and there was nothing holding her here. But what about Mother? Would it make it harder for her if she left? She would talk to her about it.

While sitting in the Bontragers' living room that morning, waiting for the service, Noah suddenly burst through the doorway and told everyone to come outside. Mattie and Mary looked at each other, wondering what could be so important.

Curiously, they walked into the yard and looked in the direction that Noah was pointing. At first Mattie couldn't see a thing. But after he mentioned a train, she suddenly saw a locomotive. She could even see the wheels turning.

"But there's no railroad over there," Father said.

"I know," Noah replied. "The closest train in that direction is about twenty-eight or thirty miles away. But it's a mirage. You know, where you can see things a long way off?"

Father nodded. He knew. He knew all about these mirages. Once he had seen people walking on the streets of Gladstone, just as though he had been there himself.

The long, hot summer passed, and Mattie was anxiously awaiting her birthday. Mother did not mind that she wanted to leave. She even encouraged her to. Mother realized that New Mexico was not a place for young people, with its harsh and often unpleasant life. She fully understood the longing in Mattie's heart to live in a settled and prosperous community—a settlement where the young people had singings and a proper social life.

So on October 28, six days after her twenty-first birthday, Mattie boarded the train at Springer, New Mexico, with Hutchinson, Kansas, as her destination. She had written Jake and Ida earlier and informed them of her schedule. She hoped they would be waiting when she arrived.

Mattie reclined on the green velvet seat of the passenger coach and watched the landscape rushing westward. Far out on the prairie, a herd of cattle slowly moved toward an unseen destination. A thick cloud of dust rose about them, and Mattie could almost feel the heat, the gritty sand, and the sharp backbones of the horses. She was glad she was an Amish girl on the train and not a cowboy on the prairie. New Mexico was for the cowboys, she thought, not for her.

As she traveled eastward, she compared the stark landscape of New Mexico with the cornfields of Kansas, neatly shocked and ready to husk. Her heart felt heavy when she thought of the life Father faced. Would he recover from the severe losses he had endured the past two years?

When the train neared Hutchinson, Mattie reached to the shelf above her and retrieved her bonnet, shawl, and purse. She straightened her back and sat stiffly, searching for familiar landmarks. Everything looked as she remembered, and yet, she couldn't recognize anything in particular. It was all strangely familiar, yet strangely new. When the train began to slow, Mattie gathered her things and waited impatiently for it to stop. She couldn't see Jake and Ida's buggy at the depot, but more than likely, they had a different horse than the one they had in New Mexico.

When she at last stepped off the train onto the wide wooden platform, she couldn't see Jake and Ida at all. But a young Amishman stood beside a buggy on the west side of the building. At first she didn't think she knew him, but the next instant she recognized him as Nettie's younger brother, Sam. He was walking toward her and smiling. She caught her breath. Surely he wasn't here to pick her up!

"Hello, Mattie," he said. He stepped onto the platform and walked to her side. His blue eyes smiled into hers and bewildered her. He no longer had a Dutchboy haircut and was strikingly handsome. And how he had grown!

"Hello, Sam," she returned his greeting.

"Jake told me you were coming, so I asked him if I could pick you up."

"Oh! Well . . . that's all right with me." She laughed nervously. Turning to pick up her suitcase and other bags, she was surprised when he reached in front of her and took them. Then he carried them to his buggy and set them behind the seat. She climbed in and waited for him to untie his horse, a dark brown mare, old and shabby. Once settled in his seat, he slapped his horse with the reins and they started for Jake's house.

Sam asked many questions about New Mexico and about Tobe and Nettie. He smiled when she mentioned their little baby, and she thought he seemed pleased that they named her Mattie.

She marveled that the little blond-haired boy she had known as Sam Knepp had matured into this soft-spoken, kindhearted young man. His hands were broad and strong as they lay idle in his lap, holding the reins loosely. His shoes were shining and clean, and he smelled fresh, with just a hint of cologne.

For a few moments she felt extremely shy and nervous, but as they talked she relaxed, and all too soon they were at Jake's home. It was a small clapboard house, neatly painted, with a little yard.

Sam carried her bags inside and stayed a few minutes to visit. Mattie felt happy, indeed, that Sam thought enough of her to want to pick her up at the depot. Before he left, he invited her to attend the singing the young people would have the following evening. She wanted to attend, but felt shy about meeting so many new people. The Reno County she had left four years earlier was not the Reno County she now saw. But she would go to the singing. Of course.

The next morning Mattie met several of her cousins, Lydia, Malinda, and Anna, who welcomed her warmly. They asked her to sit with them during the Sunday service and eat dinner with them. Soon they were visiting like old friends.

All during the singing that evening, the girls stayed by her side, introducing her to people she did not know or had not seen since they were children. Mattie was keenly aware of Sam across the room, and several times she thought he smiled at her. She liked him and wondered if he thought the same of her.

The next week was filled with getting settled at Jake's and helping Ida. By the time the next Sunday arrived, Mattie felt as though she belonged in Reno County again. Church was to be held in the North district, which required quite a long drive. She didn't think she would stay for the singing since she would need to drive home in the dark. But Malinda persuaded her to stay and promised to take her home.

That evening after the adults left, the young people gathered in the kitchen, savoring the warmth from the stove. Kerosene lanterns cast soft shadows, dancing crazily over the walls. Lydia and Mattie shared books and occasionally led in songs. Sam's clear voice rang out over the rest of the group, and Mattie wished she could sing as easily.

Suddenly she wished for a nicer dress to wear. The blue one she wore was from the fabric she and Mary had purchased in Mills, New Mexico. Now it seemed worn and drab, and she wondered how her hair looked.

More than likely Sam did not even think of her the way she thought he did. There were certainly other girls who had every hair in place, had nicer clothes, and would be happy to have him ask them for a date. She supposed he had picked her up at the depot only as a friendly gesture and did not mean anything serious about it.

After refreshments were served, Mattie went to the bedroom to get her shawl and bonnet. The room was crowded and at first she wasn't sure which were hers. Just as she found them, Malinda appeared at her elbow and whispered, "Sam wants to take you home."

"Ach!" was all Mattie could say. She thought every eye was on her and suddenly felt hot all over. What could she say? She had never had a date before and wasn't sure how to act.

"Well . . . tell him it's alright with me," she stammered.

Malinda smiled mischievously and disappeared through the doorway. Mattie turned back toward the other girls and wondered what she should do until Sam was ready to go. They all seemed aware that she had been asked for a date. She felt embarrassed and decided to wait in the kitchen. From there she could see Sam standing casually beside the door. He was wearing his coat and appeared to be waiting for her.

She twisted her handkerchief in her hand into a hard knot. Malinda came out of the bedroom and motioned to her to come outside with her. When Sam saw them coming, he opened the door and slipped out into the night. They followed and waited for him to bring the buggy to the house. When he came, Mattie bade Malinda good night, descended the steps, and walked to the gate as gracefully as possible.

Sam helped her into the buggy, then walked around his horse and climbed in beside her. He pulled an old quilt around their knees. Mattie had seen nicer lap robes, but that didn't matter. Even his donkey of a horse didn't bother her. She didn't need a racehorse to take her home. Just so it was Sam. He was the nicest person she had ever known, and his quiet manner touched an unfamiliar chord within her heart.

So this is what it's like to have a date, she thought. At first she hardly knew what to say, but soon she forgot her nervousness and they had an enjoyable time together.

The moon was nearly full, silverplating the landscape. The stones beneath the buggy wheels crunched, and occasionally a dog barked from a farmhouse. Sam's horse plodded along at an even pace, oblivious to the world. And Mattie wished Jake and Ida lived farther away so they could keep riding forever.

The house was dark when they arrived, but Mattie soon found the lamp in the kitchen and lit it, turning the wick low. She wondered what she could get Sam for a snack, then remembered a tin of cocoa in the cupboard and knew Ida would not mind if she used some to make hot chocolate. It would be delicious after their cold ride home.

They spent the rest of the evening at the kitchen table, talking about New Mexico, the death of his mother, and his father's remarriage. The impact of Katie's death had not fully registered with Mattie, being so far away, and Nettie had told them little about it. Life had not always treated Sam kindly, and Mattie thought maybe this was why he seemed older and wiser than his age would suggest.

Now Sam had a stepsister, Barbara Ann, of whom he thought highly. Mattie watched as he rubbed one hand over his knuckles, then picked up a spoon and turned it around and around. His voice rose and fell in soft tones as he spoke freely and openly of his pain and loss. Sometimes he grew humorous or changed the subject. But underneath ran a serious vein of wisdom, far beyond his years.

When the clock struck twelve, they both looked up, startled that time had flown so swiftly.

"Well, Mattie, I've sure enjoyed the evening," he said, scraping back his chair and rising to leave. His presence filled the entire room.

"So have I," she replied.

"And thank you for the hot chocolate."

"Oh, you're welcome." She stood and walked him to the door.

He stopped and rested his hand on the knob. "Would you want to have another date next Sunday night?" he asked shyly.

Warm circles chased around in her heart, and she again found it hard to speak. "Why . . . yes . . . that would be alright with me," she agreed.

"Okay. The singing will be here in our district, at David Fry's. So I'll bring you home again afterward." His blue eyes crinkled merrily at the corners, and Mattie couldn't help laughing. Everything he said seemed like a joke.

He opened the door and said softly, "Good night, Mattie."

She returned his farewell with a low "Good night, Sam," and the door shut behind him.

A minute later she heard him cluck quietly to his old horse, and the buggy was rolling down the lane and out of earshot.

Mattie blew out the lamp and felt her way through the darkness to her bedroom. If she ever felt lonely, she would remember tonight. And if she was ever discouraged, she would remember Sam. His quiet strength inspired her. She would never forget him.

17

On the Road Again

Let's WANDER AWAY," Malinda suggested.

Mattie looked at her in surprise, wondering what she meant.

"I'm tired of the same old thing."

"Okay. Let's wander away," Lydia agreed. "Where shall we go?"

"To Kalona."

Mattie's eyes opened wide. "Kalona, Iowa?"

"Yeah. Let's go with Anna. She's going up there to work, and we ought to go along." She motioned to the three of them. "I'm ready to see other country."

Mattie laughed. Never in her wildest dreams did she expect Malinda to be so daring.

"What would we do?" Lydia asked.

"Oh . . . find work. You know as well as I, that there's always some poor mother needing working girls like us. What's holding us here in Reno County anyhow?"

They looked at each other and shrugged. Mattie thought of Sam and wondered if their friendship would fade if she left. She didn't want that to happen. But really, they could always write letters. And it would be fun seeing other country.

"Nothing's holding us here," Malinda insisted.

"Yeah, let's go along," Lydia agreed. "Anna knows these people she's going to work for, and we could stay there until we get jobs."

"Okay, let's go," Mattie chimed in. She wasn't accustomed to pulling up stakes and leaving whenever she got the whim. But traveling with her cousins sounded like great adventure.

The four girls bought train tickets for Kalona, Iowa, and began preparing to leave.

The Sunday evening before their departure, Sam asked Mattie if she would write to him if he wrote to her.

"Sure, I'll write to you," she responded. His eyes searched hers as though he, too, was worrying that their friendship might end when she left.

"We'll be back," she assured him.

"I hope so." He sounded doubtful.

Mattie wanted him to believe that she would never break up, that she would never forget him, and that his feelings were more important to her than anything else. But she did not know how to put it into words. She looked down, unsure of herself.

"I know you'll have fun," he brightened.

"Oh, we will," she smiled and lightheartedly suggested that he hurry and write so she wouldn't have long to wait.

"Don't worry. I will," he responded. Then with a wave of his hand, he retreated to his buggy, leaving her standing in the doorway. She was so thankful they had been able to be together once more before she left. Deep inside, a fear that it was their last date gnawed into her very being.

Early the next morning Mattie, Malinda, Lydia, and Anna boarded the train for Iowa. Again Mattie was traveling eastward. Why the East seemed more cultivated, more exciting, more promising, was a mystery. She only knew that when she went east, good things happened.

Ed Yoder met them at the depot and took them to their home. Anna was planning to work there, and the other three hoped to get jobs as soon as possible. Ed told them of several families who needed help. He said it was up to them to decide who wanted to work where. Mattie chose to work for Ezra and Edna Miller. They had three children and a new baby, so she expected they needed help more than the other families.

When she arrived at the neat white board house, she saw three little faces peering out of the front window. She chuckled in spite of herself and knew she would have her hands full. A stout woman opened the door and welcomed her inside.

Mattie introduced herself, and the woman smiled and seemed most appreciative of her coming. She showed her the bedroom she would share with the little girls and then asked if Mattie would mind preparing the dinner. Ezra would come in from the fields soon, and she had not had time to get it started.

"Of course I can," Mattie assured her. "Just tell me what you want."

And so the routine began—just as it had so many times before when Mattie stepped into a home and restored order to chaos.

"What's the baby's name?" Mattie asked Edna.

"It's Chester," she replied.

"That's nice. Chester Miller."

Every day Mattie eagerly awaited the coming of the mailman, hoping to receive a letter from Sam. He had promised to write, and Mattie knew he would keep his promises. Even so, time seemed to drag monotonously. Baby Chester cried, the older children fussed, meals were cooked, and laundry washed.

When the letter finally arrived, Mattie caught her breath, then rushed upstairs to her bedroom where she could read it alone. It was short, but it was a letter from Sam, and that was what mattered. Mattie read and reread the letter, then turned it over, savoring this small communication with him. She would answer him tonight.

When the baby was six weeks old, Edna told Mattie she would not need her help anymore and Ezra would take her back to Ed Yoder's the next day. When they arrived at Ed's home, Mattie saw Malinda behind the house hanging the wash on the line. *She must be finished with her job, too,* she thought.

"Is Malinda here to stay?" she asked Anna as she entered the kitchen where Anna was baking bread.

"Yes, she came yesterday and is helping me today."

So Mattie crowded into the small bedroom with Anna and Malinda, sleeping on the floor beside their bed. Under other cir-cumstances, it would have been an uncomfortable arrangement, but with her cousins it was fun.

One evening Malinda suggested they leave and go to Indiana.

"To Indiana!" Anna exclaimed. "What do you want in Indiana?"

"Oh, I don't know. Just to see other country."

"But we don't know anybody there," Anna laughed.

"I have a double first cousin in Goshen," Mattie said. "Bevy Sam Miller's wife, Mary. I think it would be fun to go there for Christmas."

"Yeah, I think so too. And let's go by bus this time. I'm tired of the train," Malinda suggested.

"We'll see what Lydia says when she comes back," Mattie said.

When Lydia returned at the end of the week, she became just as excited about going to Indiana. But Anna decided to stay with the Yoders and let the other three go without her.

Before they left, Mattie wanted to get a Christmas gift to send to Sam. The next Saturday, she and the other three girls made a special trip to town to shop. They browsed through one store after another, but Mattie could not find an appropriate gift.

"Shall we pick it out for you?" Lydia asked, teasing.

"No, I'll find something yet," Mattie answered.

Finally she decided on a box of stationery, blue with a border of darker blue. She hoped he would like it. And, she grinned smugly to herself, it would be useful when writing to her.

When she arrived back at Ed Yoder's home, she carefully wrapped the box of stationery in brown paper and tied it tightly with white string. She decided not to include a return address. After she reached Goshen and knew what their plans would be, she could send that. Carefully she addressed the box and took it to the mailbox.

On Friday morning, Anna took the three girls to the bus depot in Kalona. She bade them good-bye, and Mattie wondered if she really wanted to stay or if she felt obligated to help the Yoders. They would certainly miss her.

Christmas was spent with her cousin Mary and her husband, Sam. But after the holiday passed, Malinda once more decided to move on. This time she wanted to go to Berne. It was only a few hours from Goshen, and she knew of some Swartzes who lived there. She said she had heard that the young people there did something special for New Year's, and wanted to get in on that this year. So once again, Mattie and Lydia followed, traveling by bus.

"Isn't this something?" Mattie laughed as they settled into the overstuffed seats. "I wonder what Mother would think if she knew how many places I've visited since I left New Mexico."

"She'd probably think you have itchy feet or something," Lydia replied.

"It's Malinda who has the itchy feet. She's the one who's always coming up with some new place to visit."

"It's fun, though," Malinda defended herself.

"I know it is," Mattie giggled, feeling as if she were living in the lap of luxury.

The Swartzes were surprised but glad to see Lydia and Malinda and welcomed Mattie as though she were one of them, too. When Sunday arrived and the girls went to church, they met Anna Hilty, a beautiful young girl who invited them to stay at her house. So Mattie and Malinda went with her, while Lydia stayed at the Swartzes.

"I think Lydia has a shine on Pete Swartz," Malinda told them as they traveled along the frozen gravel road in Anna's buggy. It had no top or dashboard, and even in the middle of the day, Mattie felt as though her feet were freezing.

That evening while Malinda and Anna popped popcorn and *schnitzed* (cut) apples, Mattie retreated to the bedroom and wrote Sam a long, long letter. She wrote of all they had done since leaving Iowa and of their plans to stay at Berne for a while, perhaps even getting jobs there. They didn't know.

Mattie stared at the darkened window, wondering if she should tell him that she missed him and thought a lot of him. Would he think she was too forward to write that? But it was the truth. She did think a lot of him and hoped he thought just as much of her. But what if he didn't? What if he was just being friendly?

Then she remembered the look in his eyes when they parted at Jake's home. His tenderness and sadness had touched her heart. Now she decided that, surely, he wouldn't think she was out of her place to tell him she thought a lot of him. So, after signing her name, she added a P.S. and wrote that she missed him and thought of him a lot. Then, upon a whim, wrote, "I love you."

Carefully she folded the letter and sealed it in an envelope. She put the Hiltys return address on the outside and scribbled on the back that he could send his next letter to her there. Then she wrote a second letter to Mother, telling her of her travels and giving her the Hilty address, too.

On New Year's Eve, Anna advised them to get naps in the afternoon because they wouldn't be getting much sleep that night.

"What are we going to do?" Mattie asked.

"Sing the New Year in. Have you ever done it?"

Malinda and Mattie looked at each other and laughed. They weren't up on all these things. "No. How do you do it?"

"In the middle of the night we get up and go from house to house and sing songs to the people, wishing them a happy New Year."

"Oh, that sounds like fun," Malinda squealed.

Mattie was amused. Malinda thought anything was fun.

That night they started around three o'clock, with the wind blowing its icy blasts from the north, and with no tops on their buggies and no dashboards. They and a crowd of other young people traveled slowly through the countryside, stopping at the homes of people they knew and sang for them.

Most of the people came groggily to the door and offered them something to eat and drink. But one man, with more money than time, handed them each a nickel and told them to buy themselves candy bars.

When daylight crept over the land, washing the world in light, Mattie expected they would go back to the Hilty's. But instead, they continued on, singing until the middle of the forenoon. By then, the wind had died. Her hands and feet still felt like wooden clubs and her nose like a enormous icicle.

The next week Mattie found a job helping another new mother. And just as before, the routine of keeping a household running smoothly became second nature, blurring the passing of time. Whenever she had a chance to speak with one of the Hiltys, whether at church or in town, she asked if she had received a letter.

Their answer was always the same: "No, not yet." And then they would smile and assure her that they would see to it she got it when it came.

One day, she looked up from her bread baking and saw Anna drive in the lane. Her heart quickened, knowing that at last she had received a letter. She washed her hands and hurried to the front door to invite her inside.

"Well, you got a letter, but it's not from Kansas." She handed the white envelope to her. Mattie reached for it, bitterly disappointed that it wasn't from Sam. It had no return address and was postmarked in Plain City, Ohio. Immediately she recognized Mother's handwriting. *Plain City?!* she thought.

"Sit down," she motioned to Anna. Then she ripped the envelope open. "Oh, my!"she gasped.

"What is it?" Anna questioned.

"I don't know yet." She quickly read the letter to herself and then aloud for Anna.

Dear Mattie,

We had to sell most of our things in New Mexico and are now living here at Plain City with Dawdy's. We hope to have a house of our own soon but don't know where. Dan's moved to Elkhart County, Indiana, but Tobe's plan to come here, too. Everybody is moving out of New Mexico because things have gone from bad to worse. It would be nice if you could come and spend some time with us.

Love,
Mother

Mattie sighed and a lump formed in her throat. She wasn't surprised at all to hear that everyone was leaving New Mexico. Not surprised, but very, very sad. The end of an era had passed. An era of adventure and disappointments.

All their shining hopes and dreams lay scattered among the barbed-wire fences and adobe houses. New Mexico! It had broken them all.

18

The Car

"YOU DIDN'T ACTUALLY sell all the china, did you, Mother?" Mattie asked sadly.

"We had to, Mattie," Mother answered as she sat at the kitchen table, her hands clasped tightly before her. "You don't understand. We had to get money somehow to be able to come back."

"I know, Mother. But the china was your wedding gift from Father and, well. . . . I'm sorry it went like it did out there." A lump rose in Mattie's throat and she looked away.

"Yes, I know." Mother picked at the tablecloth. "I didn't want to sell the china either, but we couldn't stay in New Mexico. We had no money to keep on farming and no money to come back East with, so we had no choice but to sell everything."

She looked out the window before adding, "We can start over again here."

Mattie knew Mother was speaking more hopefully than she actually felt. It was true that Father could get carpentry jobs to have money to live on, but it would require a lot of time and patience to set up housekeeping, with absolutely nothing to start with. *A couple their age shouldn't be destitute,* Mattie thought.

But Father, the everlasting optimist, didn't let their losses in New Mexico discourage him. He set to work and declared that soon they would have a place of their own and all would be well again.

The first Sunday Mattie attended church services in Plain City, she met a girl about her age with light brown hair, laughing gray eyes, and a quick smile.

"Who's that girl sitting at the end of our bench?" she asked Mary.

Mary leaned forward and looked down the long row of girls.

"That's Ellen Frey. She's lots of fun."

Mattie chuckled. She would like to get to know her. Maybe after church she'd have a chance to visit with her.

Not only did she have a chance to talk with Ellen Frey, but by evening they were behaving like old friends.

"Come, sit with me." Ellen pushed her toward the benches where the girls would sit during the singing. "We can talk until it's time to sing."

After they were seated, Ellen asked Mattie if she had a boyfriend.

Mattie nearly choked. Ellen was wasting no time in finding out her life history. She thought of Sam. Was he her boyfriend? She hadn't gotten a letter from him since Christmas, so apparently she wasn't his girlfriend anymore.

She had specifically told Anna to be sure to send any mail she might get to Dawdy's. Now what had happened? Had he taken offense at her last letter? That was the only reason she could think of, which might have stopped him from writing. How she regretted having written as she had!

Ellen was watching her closely.

"No, I don't," Mattie answered. Now she had admitted it, admitted what she had refused to accept before. She and Sam had broken up, and she didn't know why. Pain cut through her heart. She looked away to hide it from Ellen's wide perceptive eyes.

"Then maybe I can get a date for you tonight," she suggested.

"No, don't. Please." Mattie was not ready to date someone else.

"Why not? You said you don't have a boyfriend."

"I know. But . . . I just, um, don't want to."

"You're not shy, are you?"

"No, it's not that. It's just that . . . well . . . I don't want to tonight," Mattie insisted.

Nearly everyone was seated, and the singing would soon begin, so Ellen only smiled and opened the songbook. Mattie was relieved that she was able to pass it off so easily. None of the boys here compared with Sam, and she knew it would be a long time before she felt like dating anyone else. Only time could heal the wound in her heart.

Mattie soon had another job, working for new mothers again. She hoped she could help Father and Mother regain what they had lost. With Giddle and Mary's earnings too, and what Father earned, they soon had a house of their own. It was small, but it served the purpose.

Mother got chickens and turkeys and a few geese. Next she bought a cow and a pig, and soon she was busy planting fruit trees and tearing up a plot of ground for a garden. It wasn't long before the small place was comfortable and homey.

After Giddle turned twenty-one, he began saving his money for an automobile. The smell of gasoline and the power of an engine had always intrigued him, and now he wanted one for himself. The Amish church felt it necessary to restrict the use of the gasoline engine and did not allow automobiles. But Giddle wasn't a member of the church yet, so he was not pledged to keep the *Ordnung* (rules).

By carefully saving his money, Giddle purchased a used car. It was dark green with a gray interior. A spare tire was on the back, and luggage racks on the back fenders. It wasn't long before he was wanting to travel with his "new" car.

"When Dan Miller comes from Hutch', I'd like to see some country," he told Mattie one day.

"You mean . . . go traveling?" she asked.

"Yeah. You and Ellen ought to come with us, and we'll go to Illinois and Indiana."

"Oh, that would be fun," Mattie exclaimed. "But why not take Mary instead of Dan?"

"She's so wrapped up with Pete Miller, I doubt she'd want to go along."

"Oh, yes, she would!"

"Yeah, but then I'd be the only boy."

Mattie laughed. Well, if he wanted Dan Miller to go along, then that would be all right with her.

Several weeks later, Dan Miller from Hutchinson, Kansas, came by train to visit Giddle. Mattie listened carefully for news of Sam Knepp. Now she learned that his family had moved to Anderson County in eastern Kansas.

Was this the reason she hadn't heard from him? Had he lost the Hilty address she had sent him and didn't know that she was now in Plain City? Should she write to him again and tell him her current address? But what if he was not interested in her anymore and was dating someone else?

They hadn't dated often and written only casually, until she had told him. . . . Oh, she couldn't bear to think about it! Had she actually written that she loved him? But he didn't seem like the type to get offended easily, and she didn't think that would have stopped him from writing. Yet she couldn't be sure.

The morning Giddle, Dan, Ellen, and Mattie left, Mother asked them to please be careful. She seemed worried about their safety. They reassured her that a car was just as safe as a buggy and that the main roads were built for fast-moving traffic. They would be all right.

When they turned onto the road in front of their house, they could see her still standing at the front window, watching them leave. It gave Mattie an eerie feeling. Maybe they shouldn't go on this trip after all. But once they entered the main highway and traffic was light and orderly, her fears subsided and she enjoyed the passing scenery. Giddle seemed confident of the route he wanted to take, and Mattie paid no attention to the road signs.

Miles slipped away and the afternoon sun shone brightly through the windshield. Dan grew quiet and began to doze, his head nodding, then jerking up again. Mattie and Ellen giggled quietly each time he woke with a start.

That evening they stopped at the Hiltys in Berne, Indiana. Mattie asked if Malinda and Lydia were still in the community.

"Oh, no. They left soon after you did," Anna told her.

"Where did they go?"

"Back home. But Lydia and Pete Swartz are still going together, and I expect they'll be getting married before too long. He keeps making remarks like that, and she was terribly excited about him when they left."

"That doesn't surprise me," Mattie answered. "What about Malinda?"

"She had a few dates here, but she didn't date anybody seriously that I know of. What about you?" Anna asked.

"You know, I never heard from Sam after I left here. I had given him your address. You didn't get any letters for me, did you?"

"Why, no," Anna answered. "I thought you were still writing and he had your Plain City address."

"No, we're not. I suppose he's interested in someone else."

"Hmm. It seems strange that he didn't write and tell you he wanted to break off with you."

"Well . . . he probably wasn't as serious as I was taking him," Mattie answered.

She decided that she might as well forget about him, no matter how hard it seemed.

The evening passed quickly, and the three girls continued visiting long after the lamps had been blown out. When morning arrived, they would rather have stayed in bed a while longer. But Giddle had places he wanted to see and didn't want to be waiting on girls lounging in bed.

Mattie and Ellen dressed in the dim light of an oil lamp and packed their suitcases carelessly, anxious to get on the road where they could nestle down and sleep again. They visited friends and relatives in Goshen, Indiana, and Arthur, Illinois, before turning eastward again and starting for home.

Along the way they collected souvenirs wherever they went: salt and pepper shakers and berry dishes. The girls were each given a beautiful platter at one of the places they stayed. They packed these carefully among their clothing in the suitcase.

Instead of retracing their route through northern Indiana,

they decided to go straight across the center of the state. It was shorter and would give them the opportunity to see new country.

The sun was sinking quite low in the west when they drove into Rawleyville, a sleepy town with trolley tracks running alongside the road. After leaving town, they soon found themselves at the end of the pavement and driving on gravel.

"This isn't right!" Giddle exclaimed, pulling the map out from beneath the seat.

Dan took it from him and asked which road he wanted.

"We should have taken State Road 64 out of Rawleyville."

"Oh, yeah, I see that," Dan answered. "Turn around and I'll help you find it."

A farmhouse lay a short distance ahead, so Giddle decided to turn around in that lane. The trolley track crossed between the road and the house. He turned around in the short space between the tracks and the road because he didn't want to get into the people's lane too far. The gears ground as he shifted into reverse, and just as he backed up, the motor stalled.

"Oh, no!" Giddle groaned. "And it's almost five o'clock! I suppose the trolley will be coming through soon."

Almost before the words were out of his mouth, they heard the drumming of the trolley car approaching.

"Sure enough!" Mattie exclaimed. "Everybody out!"

"No, Mattie!" Giddle spat out the words. "The car will start again." He turned the key and the starter ground and ground helplessly, but the engine would not fire. They could see the trolley as it drew closer, rumbling down the tracks. Suddenly it blew its shrill, nerve-racking whistle.

"Come on! We have to get out or we'll all be killed!" Mattie insisted.

"No, Mattie! There's plenty of room between the tracks and the car. It's not going to hit us," Giddle shouted nervously.

"I don't care what you say, Giddle! I'm getting out!" And with that, Mattie threw the back door open and pulled Ellen out with her. Then, seeing that Dan and Giddle intended to stay in the car, she jerked the front door open and had only enough time to pull Dan out with them before the trolley, with whistle blowing and brakes squealing, hit the back of the car and smashed it against a telephone pole.

"Nooo!!!" Mattie and Ellen screamed as they stood rooted to the ground. Giddle was still in the car!

With a final screeching and shuddering, the trolley ground to a halt with the rear fender of the car still caught on its frame. The car was in pieces, and Giddle slumped lifelessly over the steering wheel.

Mattie began to cry and ran to him. The man who had been driving the trolley rushed to her side, and together they reached through the wreckage to see how Giddle was. He was breathing lightly and didn't look hurt. Slowly he raised his head, and Mattie sighed in relief.

"Giddle! Are you okay?" she asked.

He did not answer. Instead, he dropped his head onto the steering wheel again.

"Giddle! Talk to us!" she insisted.

Again he lifted his head, his eyes blank and staring.

"Are you okay?"

"Yeah," he mumbled.

"He's just dazed," the man told her. "He'll come around in a minute."

"I told him to jump out, but he wouldn't," she said. "He thought you would miss us."

"I thought so, too," the man told her. "That's why I didn't brake sooner. I didn't see until the last minute that we were going to hit. By then it was too late, and I couldn't do anything about it. I'm really sorry."

"You did what you could. If we wouldn't have missed the road back in town, we wouldn't have been here when you came through. Then all this wouldn't have happened." Mattie reached through the twisted car window again and nudged Giddle, asking if he was sure he was all right.

He turned and looked at her blankly. "What happened?" he croaked hoarsely.

"The trolley hit us."

"It did?"

"Yeah. Can you get out?"

"I don't know."

Dan and Ellen were now standing at her side. They tugged together and managed to get the car door open far enough to help Giddle out. He didn't want to put any weight on his legs at first, and they thought he might have broken something. But after a while, he began to walk around and seemed more like his natural self.

The motor was lying one hundred feet farther up the road, and pieces of the car were scattered everywhere. Their suitcases had burst open and clothes were in the road, in the yard, and even inside the trolley. The dishes they had packed so carefully were now broken and scattered. The spare tire was bent in half and lying on the trolley tracks. But they were all alive.

"Mattie, if it weren't for you, I'd be dead," Dan said.

"Me too," Ellen agreed.

"Well, I'll tell you what—when I saw the trolley coming, I decided we couldn't take any chances," Mattie told them. Her legs were still unsteady and her voice weak. How thankful she was that Giddle had been spared! By the looks of the car, it was a miracle indeed. Hardly a part was left untouched.

The couple who lived in the farmhouse came out and offered their assistance. Because they had nowhere else to go, it was decided they would stay there for the night and try to find a way home in the morning. They picked up their scattered clothing, broken dishes, and pieces of the torn and broken car and towed it into the yard. Then they solemnly ate supper, washed the dishes, and went to bed.

It was a small house and had only two bedrooms, so Giddle slept on the couch while Dan slept on the floor. Giddle looked pale and unnatural, and Mattie wished he could sleep in the bed instead of the girls. But he refused and the night passed with Mattie and Ellen sleeping in comfort upstairs.

The next morning after a delicious breakfast, they gathered in the living room to discuss their situation. They decided to pool their money and see if they had enough to buy another car.

Giddle and Dan dug into their pockets and opened their wallets, while Mattie and Ellen ran upstairs, grabbed their purses, and skipped down to the living room again.

"Here comes the gold." Dan teased them.

"No, sir!" Ellen said. "You won't find much here."

They opened their purses and counted their money. All together they had $75.00.

"Do you think we can find anything for that amount?" Mattie asked the boys.

"I think so," Giddle answered. "Let's go and see."

So the farmer took them to town, and before noon they had found a car for $80.00. It wasn't as nice as the one Giddle had wrecked, but it would get them home.

"We don't have quite enough money," Giddle told the man.

"How much do you have?" he asked.

"$75.00," Giddle answered.

"So you're five dollars short." He rubbed his chin thoughtfully, then added, "That'll be enough."

Mattie opened her purse and counted the bills and all the small change into his hands. He thanked them, and in no time at all they were back on the road in their own car.

When they reached the farmhouse again, the lady had their lunch packed so they could eat while they drove. And sitting on the table beside the lunch were two beautiful platters, one for Ellen and one for Mattie. The lady had gone to her cupboard and chosen two for them. They were overwhelmed with the couple's kindness and thanked them again and again.

As they left, driving back to the road they had missed the evening before, their hearts were full and genuinely thankful.

Now—how would they tell Mother?

19

Too Dutch

Here MATTIE WAS . . . clickety-clacking on the train again. This time Ellen was with her, heading toward New York State. Ellen had a Mennonite friend, Clara Lance, who had written and told her of a need they had for workers at a children's home. She would meet them at Buffalo and take them to the home. They were elated at the prospect of working with children.

When they arrived at the depot, Clara was waiting. After loading their suitcases and bags in her car, she expertly drove through the streets of Buffalo, turning this way and that, until they reached the outskirts of the city. There they found the countryside beautiful and serene, with rolling hills and meandering streams, quaint farms and fat cattle.

It didn't seem possible that a girl, younger than themselves, could drive a car so easily. She told of the work they would be doing and about the children there. She was sure they would enjoy it very much.

The children's home was in Williamsville. As they drove through the entrance, they saw tall red-brick buildings in every direction.

"That one over there is the Baby Fold." Clara pointed toward a building on the left. Then she turned toward another and added, "That one is the Children's Cottage."

It didn't look like a cottage at all because it was three stories high. There was another one for the older girls and one for the boys. Then there was a building for the laundry room, dining room, lounge, and office. She parked in front of the office and took Mattie and Ellen inside, where they met Mr. Smith, the administrator.

He talked about the work that was expected of them and informed them that they would work in the laundry. They agreed on a wage of $45.00 a month, which was more than Mattie had ever earned.

That evening they ate in the dining room with the children and became acquainted with a few of them. Some were shy and bashful, others were talkative. None were boisterous and ill-mannered. Mr. and Mrs. Eve, the houseparents in the Boys' Cottage, welcomed them warmly and told them they would be sleeping in an upstairs apartment in their building.

After the meal they gave the girls a tour of the home and showed them to their room. It was on the third floor at the top of a winding staircase. As they plodded up the stairs carrying their suitcases and other bags, Mattie absentmindedly counted the steps.

"Sixty-two!" she announced when they reached the top.

"Sixty-two steps?" Ellen asked.

"Yep. Sixty-two steps."

They leaned over the rail and looked down, down, all the way to the bottom floor. The kitchen was on the first floor, and they could see it through the doorway. Their bedroom was light and airy, quite bare, but comfortable nevertheless.

The next morning they began their work in the laundry, washing clothes for thirty babies, thirty children aged two to twelve years, and twenty girls and twenty-two boys aged twelve to sixteen. They scrubbed with scrubbing boards and hung everything outside on long washlines to dry.

Mattie and Ellen soon learned that it rained often in New York, and when it rained they had to hang the wash indoors. Anything was used for a drying rack if it could hold a diaper, a T-shirt, a slip, or a bedsheet. On Saturday evening they sprinkled the clothing that needed ironing and rolled it up tight to keep moist. Then on Monday morning they were ready to iron.

On Sunday everyone dressed in their Sunday best and were taken to church, where the children were quiet and reverent. When they returned to the home, they changed into everyday clothes and played in the yard from dinner until suppertime.

After the first Sunday, Mr. Smith told Mattie and Ellen that they could attend a church of their own faith if they wanted to. Because there were no Amish churches in the area, they decided to attend the Mennonite church.

"Why don't we call Clara and ask her to come and pick us up next Sunday so we can go to church with her?" Ellen suggested.

"Yes, let's," Mattie agreed.

After finishing the day's washing, they walked to the office and asked to use the telephone.

"Of course," Mr. Smith said and motioned to the telephone on the wall.

They looked at one another. "Go ahead," Mattie whispered to Ellen.

"No, you go ahead," Ellen whispered back.

"No, you do."

Neither of them had used a telephone before and they weren't sure how to make a call.

"You do."

"You do."

"No, you!"

They were trying not to giggle because Mr. Smith was just across the desk from them. So, just to save face, Mattie bravely picked up the earpiece. It was heavy and awkward. She slowly turned the crank on the side.

"You have to turn it real hard," Mr. Smith instructed her.

Mattie turned harder, but still the bell didn't sound.

"Harder than that," Mr. Smith said.

So Mattie spun the crank with all her might, and Ellen doubled over with laughter. Mattie couldn't help chuckling too, until the operator came on the line asking whom she wanted to call. Mattie quickly sobered and told her she wanted Wayne Lance.

While the telephone was ringing in the Lance home, Mattie suddenly turned cowardly. She couldn't talk to someone she couldn't see! Impulsively, she handed the earpiece to Ellen. Ellen tried to give it back, but Mattie pushed it away. She had done the first part, now Ellen could do the second.

"Hello?"

Ellen heard a voice greet her and knew that she must answer it. She put her mouth close to the mouthpiece and said "Hello," too. Then, not knowing what else to say, she asked for Clara.

"This is Clara," the voice said.

"This is Ellen," Ellen nearly shouted into the mouthpiece. She got right down to business and said, "We'd like to go to your church next Sunday and wondered if you could come and pick us up."

"Oh, sure," Clara answered. "I'll be there about nine o'clock."

"Okay. And good-bye."

"Good-bye."

With a sigh Ellen replaced the earpiece, thanked Mr. Smith, and the two hurried out of the office.

"Whew! Such an ordeal!" Ellen sighed as they stepped out onto the sidewalk. They decided they wouldn't need to use the telephone again while they were there.

Tuesday morning the nurse from the Baby Fold rushed into the laundry room and asked if either Ellen or Mattie could help her bathe the babies. Her helper had gotten sick during the night. She desperately needed help. Both girls would have enjoyed helping. Since Ellen was elbow-deep in sudsy water and Mattie was nearly finished sorting clothes, they decided that Mattie would go.

"But next time it's my turn," Ellen called after them.

When they arrived at the Baby Fold, Mattie thought there must be nearly a hundred babies crying at once.

"Take any one you want and give it a bath. There are clean clothes in the bathroom. And make sure you powder them," the nurse said as she hurried to the far end of the nursery.

Mattie saw a black baby girl peeking through the bars of her crib. She looked about nine months old and was cute as could be, bright-eyed and smiling. Mattie picked her up and took her to the bathroom. There she bathed her and put a soft blue kimono on her. Then she put her back in her crib and unknowingly placed her head at the foot end.

Mattie saw a rattle lying on the windowsill, so she picked it up and handed it to the little baby. Then she took a baby boy from the next crib and bathed, powdered, and dressed him. When she returned to the nursery to put him back in his crib, she discovered the black baby had turned herself around, with her head at the proper end, and covered herself with her blanket. She was peeking out from beneath the blanket with eyes shining.

Mattie laid the little boy down and went to her. She pulled the blanket down, "You little Betsy!" she said, shaking her playfully. The baby giggled and turned over to hide her face. Mattie laughed, covered her up again, and patted her back affectionately before hurrying on to bathe another baby.

Hour after hour she bathed, powdered, and dressed little bodies, putting each one back in their cribs for the day. How they could be so content to lie there, passing the time without entertainment of any kind, was more than Mattie could understand. She would have enjoyed playing with them and letting them sit up and crawl around. When dinnertime arrived, Mattie was sorry to leave the nursery and return to the laundry. But Ellen needed her, too.

On Friday Mattie received a letter. She looked at it curiously and saw it was from her sister Sarah. What a nice surprise! She read it immediately. After Sarah's signature, she had added a P.S., "I'm praying for you."

Sarah's praying for me, thought Mattie. It made her letter sacred. Soon she was receiving letters from Sarah every Friday. And always she ended with "P.S.: I'm praying for you." Mattie was deeply touched and hoped Sarah would continue praying for her.

Sundays were days Mattie and Ellen anticipated. Clara would pick them up in the morning, and they usually went with the

Mennonite youth to someone's house for dinner. Then they played games in the afternoon and went to church again in the evening.

One afternoon Ellen tugged at Mattie's sleeve and whispered that she had a secret to tell her.

"Whatever can it be?" Mattie asked.

"Lloyd asked me for a date tonight," she answered.

"He did? What did you say?"

"I said yes, of course," Ellen giggled.

"What are you going to do?"

"Go to church with him, and then he'll take me home. What else would we do?"

Mattie giggled with Ellen. They weren't used to the Mennonite ways. But one thing was sure: they could learn.

Ellen and Lloyd began having dates almost every Sunday night. One Monday morning while Mattie was standing at the dresser combing her hair, Ellen sat on the bed beside her, seemingly troubled.

"What's the matter?" Mattie asked.

Ellen giggled self-consciously before answering. "Well, last night just before Lloyd was ready to leave, he asked me the funniest question. He asked if I wanted to go steady. What did he mean, Mattie?"

"Why, Ellen," Mattie turned to her. "He wants you for his girlfriend all the time. You know—he wants to go steady."

"Oh, Mattie!" Ellen was horrified. "I'll bet he thinks I don't like him."

Mattie laughed. "What did you tell him?"

"I just kept saying that I didn't know. Because I really didn't, Mattie. I didn't know if I wanted to go steady or not. I didn't think I was unsteady, so why should he ask me if I wanted to go steady? I just couldn't figure him out," Ellen said.

Mattie laughed until her sides ached.

"But that's how the Mennonite people do," she explained. "They date for a while, then if they really like each other, they go steady. That means they are serious about each other. And he was wanting to go steady with you, Ellen."

"Oh, no!" Ellen wailed, covering her face. "I know he thinks I don't like him."

Mattie had fun over Ellen. But she knew that she was not above mistakes either. The Mennonite young people were so different from the Amish that the two girls often felt confused and unsure of themselves. Yet there was something genuine about their commitment to the Lord. They felt drawn to them and enjoyed every minute they spent with them.

Boys began asking Mattie for dates, too, but somehow she could not bring herself to accept them. She knew she should forget Sam, but it was hard. Finally, she agreed to have a date with Ray. He was a pleasant young man, and Mattie thought she would probably feel comfortable with him.

They had eaten dinner at Clara's home that day, and her father had asked Ray to lead in prayer before the meal. Never had Mattie heard anyone pray as he did. He spoke as though God was right in the room with them. Mattie had even opened her eyes to see if he was actually praying.

Then, in the afternoon, he had followed her to the kitchen. While they were alone, he asked if she would like to have a date that evening. Mattie said she would enjoy that. As the evening approached, her anticipation heightened. She knew that he was a true Christian and respected him highly.

Their supper was light, with only popcorn, egg sandwiches, and apple cider. Ray sat beside Mattie during the meal, and she found herself completely at ease with him. He had a quick sense of humor and made her feel special. After the dishes were washed, she excused herself to go to Clara's bedroom to freshen up. When she returned, he was waiting in the living room for her.

"Ready to go?" he asked, rising to his feet. He was tall and slim and neatly dressed.

"Yes, I'm ready," she smiled.

He held the door for her, and they stepped out into the golden evening sunshine. His car was dark blue, with hardly a speck of dust. As they rode through the countryside, he asked about her family and seemed especially interested about their life in New Mexico. Too soon they were parked in the churchyard and needed to part for the service. The women sat on one side of the meeting room while the men sat on the other. She slid onto the polished bench beside Ellen.

"So you finally did it," Ellen whispered.

Mattie only smiled. What fun to feel special!

That night as they drove the short distance to the children's home, Mattie asked about his family. They were farmers and milked cows. He said he thought farmers were doing what God intended people to do: living close to nature and seeing God in their everyday lives. Mattie had never heard that before, but it made sense to her.

When they reached the Boys' Cottage, she invited Ray inside. They went to the kitchen to get a snack. Then they sat at the table and talked about the home and the work she and Ellen did. When he was ready to leave, he stood and thanked her for the enjoyable evening.

"And when can I see you again?" he asked.

"Um . . . what?"

"When can I see you again?"

That's what Mattie thought he had said.

"Well, I don't know," she answered. She didn't know when he could see her again. Maybe he'd drive past tomorrow and see her, or maybe he wouldn't see her again until in church the next Sunday. How did she know when he'd see her again?

Ray looked away. "Well, that's all right," he said quietly.

Suddenly she grew nervous and her cheeks burned. What should she have said? She couldn't bring herself to look at him and rubbed her hand across the worn tablecloth. He turned toward the door, and she stood to follow him.

Then he smiled and thanked her for the wonderful evening. Her confidence returned, and she thanked him for bringing her home. She told him she had enjoyed it very much. He nodded and smiled, and after bidding her good night, he disappeared into the darkness.

The next morning she asked Ellen what a boy means when he asks when he can see a girl again.

"That means he wants to have another date," Ellen said.

"What?!" Mattie exclaimed.

"Did Ray ask to see you again?"

"Yes. And I thought, well, dumb . . . I don't know when he can see me again. Maybe tomorrow or maybe not until church next Sunday."

"Ohh!" Ellen screamed and flopped across the bed, in a fit of merriment until the tears came. Mattie chuckled, failing to see the humor.

Finally Ellen sat up and explained, "You see, Mattie, he wanted to have another date, and he was asking you when it would suit."

"Well, why couldn't he say it in plain words, instead of asking when he can see me again? I didn't know what he meant."

"Oh . . . we're too Dutch for these boys," Ellen groaned. "Now Ray probably thinks you don't like him either, the way Lloyd thinks I don't like him."

So the laugh was on Mattie this time. But at least they now knew what a boy meant if he asked to go steady or to see them again.

One day Mattie received a letter from Mother telling her of Mary and Pete's marriage. Mattie was shocked. She didn't know they were engaged. Mother said they had decided it suddenly, and she guessed they thought they might as well go to a justice of the peace and forget about all the work of a wedding.

"They think it's a big joke," she wrote. "But I think Mary's too young to know what she actually did. Right now she's on cloud nine though. Let's hope she stays there."

Mattie chuckled. That sounded like Mary! Just go to the justice of the peace and forget about the work of a wedding! At seventeen, she was too young to know better.

One night Ellen was out late with another boy, and Clara had brought Mattie home to the Boys' Cottage. Everything was quiet when Mattie entered the front door. She tiptoed to the stairway so she wouldn't waken anyone. Softly she began the sixty-two-step climb to their bedroom.

Her shoes were clicking noisily and she stooped to take them off. She had the first shoe in her hand and was reaching down to take off the other one when she heard what sounded like a gunshot in the kitchen. Badly frightened, she jumped and nearly fell. Not bothering to take off her other shoe, she raced up the stairs as fast as she could, clumping loudly.

She reached the second landing, slowed, and was planning to take off her other shoe when there was a second loud "BANG!!" Away she went again, clumping all the way to the third floor. There she gathered enough courage to look over the side of the banister, and just as she did so, there was a third "BANG!!" Turning, she burst through their bedroom door, dived into bed, pulled the blankets over her head, and hoped whoever was shooting wouldn't find her.

For two hours she lay still as death, with one shoe on and one shoe off, hoping that Ellen would soon come home and at the same time hoping that she wouldn't. But just a few minutes before midnight she heard soft footsteps padding up the stairway. Was it Ellen? Or was it a murderer? The bedroom door opened and Ellen stepped in.

"Ellen!" Mattie sat up in bed. "Are you all right?"

"Of course! Are you?"

"Didn't you see anything downstairs?"

"No, was I supposed to?"

"I heard three gunshots in the kitchen when I came home."

"You did?"

"Yes!"

"Are you sure?"

"Of course I'm sure!"

"It was probably something else. I didn't hear or see anything unusual when I came in."

But Mattie could not believe that it had not been something out of the ordinary. She knew what she had heard, and she had heard shots in the kitchen. The next morning they asked Mrs.

Eve if they had heard anything the night before.

"It was around ten o'clock," Mattie told her.

"That was soon after we went to bed, and we didn't hear a thing. But I'll ask around and see if anyone else heard it," she said.

That afternoon Mrs. Eve stepped into the laundry. Mattie and Ellen were both ironing, which was a warm job in the winter and a hot job in the summer. Sweat was streaming down their faces.

"I found out who was shooting in the kitchen last night, Mattie."

"You did?"

"Yes. It was some eggs."

"What do you mean, it was eggs?"

"The cook left three eggs on the stove for the night watchman. She thought the coal was nearly burned up and would be just warm enough to cook those eggs slowly. By the time the night watchman was planning to come through and check on things at midnight, they were supposed to be ready. But the stove must have been hotter than she thought because they cooked dry and exploded. They're even splattered on the ceiling."

"Oh, my! That ceiling is high!" Mattie exclaimed. "It must be at least twelve feet high."

Mrs. Eve gave her a motherly smile and told her to wake them up the next time it happened.

"I couldn't have. I was too scared," Mattie said. "But I'm glad to know it was eggs and not somebody out of their mind."

As time passed, Mattie was called more and more to help with the children. Mr. and Mrs. Eve went on vacation the middle of October and left Mattie in charge of the boys. Every morning each one hung their pajamas and robe on a hook beside their bed and made their beds neatly. Next, they swept the floors. Not until everything was in place and shining clean did they go outside to play or work in the garden.

One morning while she was working in the Boys' Cottage, Ellen entered the front door. She looked as though she had been crying.

"I'm ready to go home," Ellen announced woefully.

"Oh, no, Ellen! I'm having a good time."

"But I'm tired of this and want to go home," Ellen insisted.

"What happened?"

So the sad story spilled out and many tears with it. The nurses from the Baby Fold had needed some clothes over the weekend and came into the laundry and messed everything up. Wet clothes were hung over dry ones, and they had taken all the clothes that Mattie and Ellen had sprinkled and folded on Saturday and pulled them apart. Some of them were dry and some were wet.

To make matters worse, Mr. Smith had come into the laundry that morning and told Ellen not to put wet clothes on top of dry ones. Ellen had been too upset to tell him the nurses had done it. So now she wanted to go home, and right away.

"Oh, my. I'm not ready to go home yet," Mattie said. "Why don't we wait until Mr. and Mrs. Eve come back?"

"But will you go then?" Ellen asked.

"I guess so. If that's really what you want to do," Mattie said.

"It's what I want to do," Ellen answered quietly.

"Then we'll go," Mattie agreed.

Mattie loved New York and loved the children. But if it was time to go home, then she was ready. It would be nice to be with their families again and to go to their own church. Home was still the best place to be, and maybe it was time they returned.

20

The Letters

MATTIE GROANED MISERABLY and rolled over in her bunk. The violent up and down and back and forth motion nauseated her to the very pit of her stomach. It was a mystery to her why she and Ellen had thought it would be fun to go home by ship.

They had taken the last ship to sail before winter out of Buffalo, New York, and were sailing through Lake Erie, bound for Cleveland, Ohio. It was a miserable journey. The cabins were small and stuffy. And now when Mattie needed a chamber pot, it was too dark to find it.

She sat up and bumped her head on Ellen's bunk overhead. Suddenly the supper they had enjoyed in the dining hall only hours earlier threatened to come up. She staggered to her feet and fell against the wall, accidentally kicking the porcelain chamber pot and sending it skittering across the floor. Grabbing it, she retched and vomited.

How she wished Ellen would wake up so she could help! The ship pitched and rolled, and Mattie fell back into her bunk. She lay still until she needed to vomit again. She was sweating profusely and gasping for fresh air. Lightning flashed through the tiny porthole and for brief seconds lit their cabin.

Suddenly Ellen sat up and half fell from her bunk. "Where's the pot?" she mumbled. A violent roll of the ship sent her sprawling across the floor and crashing against the metal door beside Mattie.

"Over here," Mattie said and weakly reached for it. It was no longer where she had left it, and she hardly had the strength to get up to find it. She waited for a flash of lightning.

"Hurry up," Ellen gasped.

Mattie felt around with her foot, and when she touched it, quickly pushed it toward Ellen. But because it was pitch dark, Ellen could not see it.

"It's there by your foot," Mattie mumbled and flopped weakly back onto her bed.

Ellen grabbed it and vomited. Then she lay on the floor, waiting for her strength to return. Never had either one felt so very sick—sick to the core of their beings. And to make matters worse, they knew they were doomed to stay on the ship until noon the next day.

The ship tossed and pitched, first one direction, then the opposite. Up and down and back and forth until Mattie wondered if they were going backward instead of forward. The chamber pot was spilling dreadfully, and Ellen needed to get off the floor.

She grabbed the side of Mattie's bed and attempted to pull herself up, but the tossing of the ship made it impossible. Mattie held her arms to keep her from slipping and together they managed to get her into a sitting position. Her gown was soaked.

"Take off your gown and wrap up in this sheet," Mattie mumbled. She pulled the sheet off her bed and helped Ellen get undressed and wrapped in it. Then they both flopped onto Mattie's tiny bunk and lay still, too weak to move.

When would this nightmare end? Would it soon be daylight? Would the waters be smoother when they got closer to land? Would their thirst for adventure be satisfied now? Whew! Mattie was too dizzy to think.

Thunder boomed outside. The ship zoomed up a mountain of water, then fell hard into a pit on the other side. Up another mountain and into a deeper pit. More thunder. More pitching back and forth. More vomiting. More changing of sheets. More exhaustion.

With time, the peaks and valleys lessened and the thunder grew distant. Mattie fell asleep and when she awoke, Ellen was back in her own bunk and the sea was nearly calm. Rolling over, she fell soundly asleep. When she woke again, sunlight was streaming through the tiny window, and Ellen was dressed and cleaning the floor.

"What a night!" she exclaimed, sitting up in bed. The sheets were pulled off the mattress and twisted around her. Everything was in disarray.

"It was awful!" Ellen agreed.

"We'll never do this again, will we?"

"Absolutely not! If I ever get off this boat, I'll never get on another one. NEVER!" Ellen declared.

Mattie chuckled and tried to stand, but her legs shook.

"Let's hurry up and go on the deck. I can't stand it down here a minute longer," Ellen said. She grabbed Mattie's suitcase and helped her get dressed. Then she tried combing her hair for her.

"Ach! I can do that," Mattie took the comb and began hurriedly combing out the snarls. When she was finally ready to go outdoors, Ellen nearly pushed her up the steps. She was in a hurry, and Mattie didn't blame her.

Other passengers were walking on the deck. Many of them clung weakly to the railing, their faces drawn and pale. They apparently had suffered through the night, too. Mattie and Ellen drank in the fresh air and sunshine. Now they wanted to reach land as swiftly as possible.

Far, far away on the horizon was a thin sliver of land. But hour after hour it failed to get closer. They rested on deck chairs, waiting impatiently for their journey to end. The sun rose higher and higher, providing cozy warmth if they were out of the wind. They laid back in their chairs, eyes closed. Whether or not they slept they didn't know.

At last they heard the engines slow and they looked up. The sliver of land was approaching fast, and tall buildings could easily be seen. Could it be that their miserable journey was nearly at an end? Quickly they went down to their bunks to get their bags and suitcases and carried them up to the deck. They didn't want even one minute of delay in getting on solid ground.

When they finally were off the ship, off the dock, and through the terminal, they walked to the Cleveland bus station several blocks away and bought tickets for Plain City. Plain City! It would be so good to be home.

Giddle picked them up at the bus depot in Plain City and was full of questions about New York, the children's home, the Mennonite young people, and the ship ride. But the girls were almost too tired to answer. When he asked how they liked the ship, both of them responded in no uncertain terms: "Please, please, don't mention it!" It would be a long time before they would be in a mood to tell of their wonderful ship ride.

It was good to be home. Oh, it was *so* good to be home! Mother was the picture of health and seemingly enjoying every minute at Plain City. For so many years she had had little contact with her sisters and Dawdy's, and now it was truly a blessing to be neighbors.

Tobe and Nettie had moved two miles to the east of them. They now had two more children, Katie and a new baby, Levi. The older children often ran through the fields to borrow a cup of sugar, bring a letter to Mother, or to help with her gardening.

One day John and Crist appeared at the front gate with a letter. They handed it to Mattie.

"Is it for me?" she asked in surprise.

"No. But Mom thought you would want to read it, too. Uncle Sam sent it to Mom."

Mattie caught her breath. *What could it be about? Was he married to someone else? Was that what Nettie thought she should know?*

Hiding both her fear and excitement, she invited them inside for cookies and lemonade. Mother bustled out of her bedroom where she had been sewing a vest for Crist.

"You're just the person I want to see," she told him. "When you're finished filling up that little belly, I want you to try on this vest." Then she turned to Mattie and asked what they had brought.

"It's a letter from Sam, and Nettie thought I would want to read it. I wonder why." She cautiously slid the letter from the envelope and scanned over its contents. Seeing nothing to cause alarm, she began reading and learned that he was planning to come to Plain City for Christmas. He didn't mention another girl or anything, so maybe he was still single and interested in her.

Hope rose within her. Sam was coming, and he wasn't married, and he apparently didn't have a girlfriend.

"What does it say?" Mother asked.

"He's coming for Christmas," Mattie answered.

"Yeah, we knew that, but Mom told us not to tell you," John said importantly, grinning from ear to ear.

"That's right, Aunt Mattie! Mom told us not to tell, and we didn't, did we?" Crist nodded.

"You sure didn't. You kept that secret like big boys!" She patted him on the head. Then her eyes met Mother's and they smiled. Mother understood perfectly.

Lydia was working away, so Mattie decided to get a job, too. Edna and John Miller needed help, and Mattie began working there. Time passed slowly since she knew that Sam would be coming for Christmas.

But when he arrived, Mattie suddenly felt shy and apprehensive. He hadn't come to see her. Maybe he wasn't interested in her at all.

The first Sunday Sam was there, she saw him walk across the porch and enter Benjamin Yoder's home. This was where they were having church services, and she was just driving into the lane when he entered the house. He was more handsome than she remembered, and her heart began hammering wildly.

Mattie entered the house through the kitchen and slipped quietly into place across the room from him. He looked up and their eyes met. He smiled and she quickly looked away.

He smiled! she thought. *He smiled at me! Why didn't I smile back?* The next time their eyes met, she smiled in return.

That evening after the singing, Sam told Ellen to ask Mattie if she wanted to have a date. Ellen hurried to the bedroom where Mattie was putting on her shawl and bonnet.

"Sam told me to ask you if you wanted to have a date tonight," she whispered excitedly.

"Shh! Everybody will hear you," Mattie reprimanded her. "Are you sure you're not making that up?"

"I'm sure! He really likes you, Mattie, I can tell. I bet he just lost your address, like I always told you he did. And here you've been so stubborn all this time and insisted that he has another girl. Now go out there and let him take you home." Ellen's eyes were shining.

"Okay," she giggled, picking up her bonnet and settling it on her head.

That night she and Sam talked and talked and talked, well past midnight. His silence had indeed been a mistake, one that neither of them could have avoided.

"I didn't know what had happened," he told her. "I got that box of stationery from you at Christmas, but you said you didn't know where you were going after that, and I never heard from you again. I figured you had found another boy you liked better and forgot about me."

"I wrote a letter from Hilty's in Indiana. Didn't you get it? I had given you my address there."

"No, I never got a letter from Indiana," he answered.

"I had written something in that letter I sent from Hiltys that I figured you didn't like and so you decided to drop me. I just knew that you had another girl and maybe had even married."

"Oh, no, Mattie. I never got that letter. What did you write that you thought I wouldn't like?"

"Oh . . . ." She was embarrassed to tell him. "I had written how much I miss you and that I hoped you missed me too . . . and some other stuff." It sounded silly now.

He threw back his head and laughed until Mattie was afraid he'd wake Father.

"Well, well, well! You didn't have to worry. I wouldn't have quit writing you because of that." He looked into her eyes affectionately.

That night before he left, he asked for a date the next Sunday night. They would make up for lost time. It had been exactly a year since they had heard from each other, and a long year it had been.

Winter passed into spring and spring into summer. Letters passed between Sam and Mattie, and all was right with the world again. She continued working for Edna and John and going home for the weekends. One day she received a letter from Sam stating that he was planning to come in June and stay for a few weeks. How her heart sang, and her work no longer seemed as work!

This time he came by bus, and she met him at the depot alone. It was a happy buggy ride home.

"I thought I might stay at your house this time, if you don't mind," he said.

"Oh, that will be just all right," she answered.

"Tobe's are so crowded and I thought that maybe Giddle won't mind too much if I barge in on him for a while. I'd like to work with your dad, too, if he needs help."

She smiled, pleased to hear that he enjoyed her family. "Father would like that very much, I'm sure."

It was a busy time with gardening and canning, so Mattie did not ask to have time off from her job as she would have liked while Sam was there. They would see each other on the weekends.

Wednesday evening Mattie was surprised to see Sam drive in John's lane in Father's buggy. She hurried out to the gate to meet him. To have him visit in the middle of the week was unusual, and she wondered if something had gone wrong at home.

"Hi," she greeted him. "Is something wrong?"

"Yeah," he answered soberly.

Her heart quickened in fear. "What's the matter?"

"I miss you," he smiled mischievously.

"Oh, you!" she laughed. "You scared me."

He chuckled good-naturedly and asked if she wanted to go for a ride. "Of course!" she cried. "Just wait a few minutes while I get the kitchen clean."

She rushed indoors and hurriedly put the dried dishes back in their places. Then she ran to her bedroom to change into a clean dress.

When she stepped into the buggy, he commented on her fast movements. "Nobody can work around you, I see."

"Especially not when someone is waiting to take me for a ride," she responded happily.

They rode throughout the countryside, talking of the happenings at home, the work at John's, and finally of their inner feelings. More and more they bared their hearts to each other.

Every Wednesday evening after that he came for a drive through the country. They just drove, talking and laughing, and then he would take her back to John's. On Sunday nights they had real dates, with him taking her to the singings and back home again.

The night before he was scheduled to leave for Kansas again, he began talking about their relationship and what it meant to him.

"I don't want to leave, Mattie, but Dad needs me," he began. "I've never enjoyed another three weeks in my life as much as I have these past three. Your family is quite different from mine, you know."

She nodded. Life wasn't the same in the Knepp home since Katie had died. Nobody can replace one's mother, and Mattie realized it was painful for Sam.

"I'm going to miss you, Mattie. Thanks so much for all you've done for me."

"Oh, Sam, I didn't do that much. If I did, it didn't seem like much because it was for you."

"I wish I wouldn't have to leave." He became more intense. "I'd like to just stay here always." Then, as though it were an afterthought, he added, "Maybe I can someday."

"Well, maybe so." Mattie looked at her hands, not knowing exactly how to answer him.

He took a deep breath and looked at the darkened window, then stood. She arose too and their eyes met. Tears glistened in his and Mattie looked away. How tender he was and she knew that he experienced much pain in his heart. Sometimes it just had to come out. She moved to his side and said, "I'll be thinking about you."

"Thank you, Mattie. You mean a lot to me, and I don't want anything to come between us. You don't know what it did to me when I didn't hear from you anymore last year. It was like something died inside of me. I had had such high hopes for us, and it seemed like they were all over."

"It was the same for me, Sam. I had a date with another boy in New York, but it just wasn't the same."

They walked through the living room to the bedroom door. He stood with his hand on the doorknob to Giddle's room.

"We won't let that happen again, will we? We know each other better now," he smiled.

"*Now* I can tell you how I feel, can't I?" she asked playfully.

"Of course. I won't mind." He laughed. "Well, we need to get to bed. Good night, Mattie."

"Good night, Sam."

Reluctantly they parted, knowing in their hearts that they were secure in each other's love.

21

Where the Pretty Moon Goes

MATTIE QUICKLY SURVEYED the kitchen and dining room to make sure no job was left undone. She did not want Edna to have extra work over the weekend. Satisfied that all was clean and in order, she hurried upstairs to her bedroom to pack her few belongings.

She and Lydia were both planning to be at home for the weekend. The times were rare that the two sisters were there together, and they enjoyed every minute of it. Mattie threw a soft shawl over her shoulders, picked up the worn brown satchel, and went downstairs to wait for John to bring the buggy to the house. Edna bustled into the kitchen with the baby wrapped warmly in a cotton blanket.

"I declare, Mattie, I don't know how you manage! Here you shucked corn this morning, and now you have the house looking so nice. Here"—she thrust two and a half dollars into Mattie's hand. "You do plan to come back Monday, don't you?"

"Oh, yes. I'll come back as long as you need me," Mattie replied. "I'd be working for someone else if I weren't working for you. It doesn't seem like I get much time at home anyhow."

Just then five-year-old Melvin burst through the door and told Mattie that his father was ready to take her home.

"May I go along?" He looked pleadingly into his mother's eyes.

"I guess so. But be sure you help carry Mattie's things," she instructed him.

"Yipp-e-e-e!" he yelled, racing out the door and across the

porch. But just as he bounded off the steps, Edna stopped him and reminded him to go back and get Mattie's satchel.

"Oh, yes. I forgot," he grinned sheepishly. He retraced his steps, entered the kitchen again, grabbed the satchel, and started for the buggy. John was waiting at the gate, and soon they were on their way. A solitary star hung low and bright in the west.

"A diamond, Melvin." Mattie pointed to the star. "Don't you think the star looks like a diamond?"

"Uh-hum." Melvin nodded. His eyes were wide, full of wonder and childlike innocence.

Corn shocks stood tall in the fields, and the fiery sunset with the bright star created a beautiful harvest scene. Only the steady clip-clop of the horse's hooves and the crunching of the buggy wheels in the gravel could be heard.

When they arrived at her home, Melvin dutifully carried the satchel to the door for her. She thanked him, waved good-bye, and stepped inside.

The comfortable warmth and light of the house dispelled all the tiredness Mattie had felt the past week. Lydia skipped down the stairs to greet her.

"Where is everyone?" Mattie inquired. She untied her bonnet and laid it on the kitchen table.

"Outside choring," Lydia answered. "So what's the news?"

"Oh, nothing really. Unless you call washing dishes, shucking corn, milking cows, and scrubbing dirty faces *news*, then I have lots of it. What's yours?"

"Nothing either. I just came home, too, and haven't talked to anyone yet."

"Did you get any mail?" Mattie asked.

"Oh, yes, I forgot to tell you." Lydia squealed in delight. "You got a letter from Sam."

"How could you forget?" Mattie exclaimed. "Where is it?"

"Right here." Lydia scampered to the cupboard and picked up a handful of papers. Shuffling through them, she picked Sam's letter from the rest and held it up to the light. "Uh-oh. It looks like he wants to break up," she said woefully.

"Oh, he does not!" Mattie reached for the letter, but Lydia jerked it away and pretended to read through the envelope.

"That's right. I read that wrong. He really says he wants to get married."

"Lydia!" Mattie rose to her feet, so Lydia quickly handed it to her to avoid a mad scramble.

The envelope was postmarked November 12. Mattie looked at the calendar. It was now the twenty-third. Just then Mother entered the kitchen, egg basket in hand and cheeks rosy from the chilly autumn air.

"How long has this letter been here, Mother?" Mattie asked.

"Oh—since about the first of the week," Mother replied.

"Well, I wish you would have sent it over to John's sometime. Sam will think I've forgotten about him by the time he gets a letter back from me."

Lydia shook her head sadly and murmured, "Poor, poor Sam."

"Well you are just *unleidlich* (unbearable) tonight." Mattie swung her bonnet at her. "I think I'll find better company."

She opened the door to the stairway, ran up the stairs, and flopped carelessly across her bed. Mattie scanned over the envelope and noticed each carefully penned letter. *He sure writes neater than other boys,* she thought. She tore it open and slid the letter from it. Unfolding the paper, she read:

Dear Mattie,

Greetings to you in Jesus' name. I hope this finds you well and happy. We have all our crops harvested now and I have enough money for a train ticket to Plain City. I thought if it suits you, I would come for Christmas and stay for several weeks again. Let me know if this is alright with you.

I've been thinking a lot about what we talked about last June and hope you have too. I miss you. Ha!

Sincerely,
Sam

P.S.: I'm very anxious to see you again.

"Oh, Sam," Mattie whispered, dropping her head on the pillow. "I'm anxious to see you too." She lay deep in thought for a long while before realizing that darkness had fallen and the family was probably ready to eat supper. Rising from the bed, she folded the letter, slid it back into its envelope, and laid it in the top drawer of the bureau.

The evening passed quickly with much visiting, teasing, and laughter. On Saturday, Lydia, Mattie, and Mother cleaned the house and baked many pies and cookies for the coming week. After the dinner dishes were washed, Mother decided to take the buggy and visit Nettie and the children. When she returned several hours later, she announced that Tobe, Nettie, Pete, and Mary were coming for supper.

"Lydia, please go down in the cellar and bring up that ham. We'll have some of that to go with potato soup," Mother instructed. "And Mattie, you may start peeling potatoes."

Excitement filled the air as Mother and the girls prepared the meal. They enlarged the table with extra leaves to make room for fourteen people. After all was in readiness, they went to the barn to do the chores. With so many hands to help, it would not take long.

When Tobe, Nettie, and their five children arrived, the noise began almost before the buggy rolled to a stop. Only when everyone bowed their heads to pray before the meal did they quiet down. But then, just as soon as it ended, their voices rose once more like a chorus of crickets on a summer night.

Mother dipped the thick soup, made of rich milk and potatoes, into each one's bowl. Tobe held little Katie's bowl up to the kettle for Mother to fill."

"Don't make it too full. I don't think she's too hungry tonight," he said. Suddenly his eyes met Mattie's and began twinkling mischievously.

"Well, what's wrong with you?" Mattie asked.

Tobe set the bowl down in front of Katie and purposely took his time breaking crackers into her soup. While Mattie waited for an answer, Giddle picked up her bowl and passed it to Mother.

"Don't make Mattie's too full 'cause I don't think she's very hungry tonight," he teased.

"*Ach, git!* (Oh, get away!)" Mattie grabbed her bowl from Giddle and waited for Mother to fill it.

"Well, you were just sitting there daydreaming, so I decided to help you. Otherwise, you wouldn't get anything to eat."

"I was just waiting for Tobe to tell me what's so funny!" Mattie replied.

"We heard some things about you and wondered when the wedding will be," Tobe said, still grinning.

Mattie broke crackers into her soup and helped little Mattie with her ham.

"Are you getting married, Aunt Mattie?" the little girl asked, looking trustingly into her eyes.

"No, Mattie, child. Some people have big imaginations."

"When is Sam planning to come?" Mary asked.

"Sometime before Christmas. I don't know exactly when," Mattie answered.

"Then you better start baking the cakes, if you know what's good for you." Tobe continued to tease.

"Ach! They'd be all spoiled by the time I get married," she countered.

"Then you'd better hurry Sam up," he insisted.

"Yeah. Spoiled cake—spoiled bride," Giddle joined in.

Mattie broke into a hearty laugh and added, "And no cake—no bride!"

After the meal was finished and the dishes washed, they gathered around the stove to visit. Only one lamp glowed beside Father, creating a cozy atmosphere. The chatter of the children quieted to a soft murmur and the adult voices became solemn and low.

Two-year-old Levi fell asleep in Nettie's arms. Katie and little Mattie nestled in their grandparents' soft ample laps. Mother stroked Katie's hair away from her face and tucked stray strands behind her ear. Mattie savored the peaceful scene. Someday things would not be as they were now, and she wished this peaceful evening would never end.

She thought of Sam and knew he would enjoy an evening like this. One by one the children fell asleep, so Nettie suggested they go home. Mother and the girls helped bundle the little ones and carried them to the buggy. After the usual "Thanks for the good supper" and "Good night," Tobe and his family and Pete and Mary departed.

Long weeks passed and Mattie received another letter from Sam asking her to pick him up at the place where the train stopped at Plain City. It was not a regular depot, but just a place in the country where it loaded and unloaded passengers. The train was scheduled to arrive at midnight on December 21.

He planned to stay for two weeks, so Mattie asked Edna if she could do without her during that time. She wanted to be at home while Sam was there. The Sunday evening before his arrival, Mattie took Ellen aside at the singing and asked her to go with her to pick Sam up.

"When is he coming?" Ellen asked, her eyes wide and twinkling merrily.

"At midnight Friday night," Mattie told her.

"Midnight!" Ellen giggled. "How romantic!"

"Yes," Mattie chuckled. "I just wish the moon were full."

"Oh, well. We'll need lanterns anyhow. Make sure you bring enough blankets in case the train is late," Ellen reminded her.

"Okay," Mattie agreed. "I'll plan to pick you up at eleven o'clock, and we should be back by one. Tell your mom not to worry."

Friday night after everyone else had gone to bed and the house was dark, Mattie departed alone. Only a small slice of the moon shone, weakly illuminating the landscape and casting eerie shadows across the road. Mattie felt a little afraid. But after Ellen joined her, the fears disappeared and the two snuggled up in their blankets for a pleasant midnight ride.

Mattie stopped the buggy a little way from the railroad, and they chatted while waiting.

Just before twelve o'clock they began feeling a small vibration in their ears. Mattie stepped out of the buggy and held Nellie's bridle. Showers of sparks flew from the screeching wheels, and with a terrible bumping and banging, the train slowed to a crawl, then rolled to a stop with the door of the passenger car in the center of the crossing. Mattie wondered how one person could possibly control so massive a machine.

Suddenly a door opened, and there stood Sam, suitcase in hand. Ellen came around the side of the horse and offered to hold the bridle if Mattie wanted to greet Sam. Mattie hurried up the road. Even in the darkness she could see the joy on his face as they drew closer.

"Mattie!" he greeted her fondly.

"Sam! It's so good to see you." She laughed lightly.

"And it's good to see you, too," he said, looking tenderly into her eyes.

Many unspoken emotions passed between them as they walked back to Ellen and the waiting buggy.

"I hope you didn't get too cold waiting for me," he said. "Who's with you?"

"Ellen. I didn't want to come alone this time of the night."

"Yes, I'm glad she did."

"Hi, Sam," Ellen greeted him as they neared the buggy.

"Hi, Ellen. It's sure nice of you to come along so Mattie didn't have to come alone," he said.

"Oh, I don't mind."

They climbed into the buggy, and Sam picked up the reins. Not until they were a safe distance away did the train start up again, and soon it was only whisper in the distance.

After leaving Ellen at her home and bidding her good night, Sam turned the buggy around to go home. Now it was only the two of them, and time seemed to stand still as they spoke softly to each other. No longer was the night frightening, and even the moon seemed to shine brighter. Occasionally their laughter filled the night air, and Sam delighted in Mattie's joyful spirit.

The next day was filled with the usual Saturday work of baking and cleaning house. Sam worked alongside Father and

Giddle as though he belonged in the family. That evening Mother prepared a simple meal of tomato soup and hamburgers. Pete and Mary came while they were eating, and soon the house was filled with laughing voices and everyone talking at once.

Mattie sensed that the family admired Sam almost as much as she. After supper Lydia offered to do the dishes, so Mattie and Sam could spend time together.

"Oh, that's nice," Sam complimented her. "But I suppose tomorrow night you'll want Mattie to do the dishes so you can spend time with—what's his name? Eli Kauffman?"

Lydia expertly flicked a towel at him, snapping him on the arm. "I can see you're not very smart," she replied.

"It's Henry Stutzman who's after her," Mattie informed him.

"Oh, well, Kauffman and Stutzman are nearly the same, so I was almost right," Sam insisted.

"Not by a long shot!" Lydia snorted, turning to the sink.

Sam looked at Mattie and asked if she would like to go for a buggy ride.

"In this cold?!" Mary asked.

"Oh, we'll stay warm," Mattie replied.

Sam hitched Nellie to Father's buggy and brought it to the house while Mattie gathered quilts and bundled up in her winter wraps. After climbing into the buggy and covering themselves with the quilts, they drove out the lane and turned to the west. The sliver of moon shone liquid and silver.

"Do you know what that kind of moon always reminds me of?" Sam asked.

"Of the song about the moon having two horns so sharp and so bright?" she guessed.

"Yes. Do you know it?" he turned to her.

"Oh, yes. Let's sing it."

So together they sang:

Oh, Mother, how pretty the moon looks tonight;
She was never so lovely before.
    Her two little horns

Are so sharp and so bright;
I hope she'll not grow anymore.

If I were up there with you and my friend,
I'd rock in it nicely, you see;
    I'd sit in the middle
    And hold by both hands.
O what a bright cradle 'twould be!

I would call to the stars to keep out of the way,
Lest we should rock over their toes.
    And there I would rock
    Till the dawn of the day,
And see where the pretty moon goes.

And there we would stay in the beautiful skies,
And thru the bright clouds we would roam,
    We would see the sun set,
    And see the sun rise,
And on the next rainbow come home.

A comfortable silence fell between them as each was lost in thought. Millions of stars twinkled brightly overhead. The crisp air purified the landscape as they traveled slowly, sometimes talking, but mostly just quietly enjoying each other's company.

"You know, Mattie," Sam began. "Your home is so different from mine. You can have fun and take things more lightly than we do. I want our home to be like that, so full of happiness."

Our home? Mattie thought. But she remained silent, for she sensed he had more to say.

He looked at her tenderly before adding, "I'd like to get married, Mattie, and I don't want anyone else for a wife but you."

"Oh!" was all she could say.

"Will you marry me, Mattie?"

She cleared her throat before answering in a low voice, "Of course I'll marry you, Sam. There's nobody else I would want for a husband than you either." Quick tears pricked her eyelids.

The buggy wheels whirled on and occasionally a dog barked, but Sam and Mattie were oblivious to everything except the future they envisioned together—always together.

The moon slid toward the horizon, turning from silver to gold to bronze.

> We'd call the stars to keep out of the way,
> Lest we should rock over their toes. . . .

Mattie began singing softly and Sam joined in.

> And then we would rock
> Till the dawn of the day,
> And see where the pretty moon goes . . .
> And see where the pretty moon goes.

The Author

Jewel Miller with her grandmother,
Martha Borntrager Knepp

J EWEL MILLER was raised at Macon, Mississippi, the daughter of Edwin and Tressa Knepp. She is married to Mervin Miller and they have four children: Jay, Marilyn, Phyllis, and Sherri Lou.

Miller is a homemaker and her many interests include photography, quilting, and handcrafts.

Along with her love for writing articles and stories, she enjoys reading classical literature and writing poetry, for which she has won numerous awards.

Much of this book was inspired by her grandmother, Martha Borntrager Knepp, who is an avid and skilled storyteller.

Jewel and Mervin Miller are members of Magnolia Mennonite Church of Macon.